SpringSong ❧ Books

Andrea   Kara

Anne   Kathy

Carrie   Leslie

Colleen   Lisa

Cynthia   Melissa

Erica   Michelle

Gillian   Paige

Jenny   Pamela

Jessica   Sara

Joanna   Sherri

Tiffany

Erica

Eileen Pollinger

BETHANY HOUSE PUBLISHERS
MINNEAPOLIS, MINNESOTA 55438

Erica
SpringSong edition published 1996
Copyright © 1985
Eileen Pollinger

Published by Bethany House Publishers
A Ministry of Bethany Fellowship, Inc.
11300 Hampshire Avenue South
Minneapolis, Minnesota 55438

Printed in the United States of America.

Library of Congress Catalog Card Number 84-73384

ISBN 1–55661–899–9   CIP

To Ruth Hanno

My mother, who shared her love for reading with me.

EILEEN POLLINGER is a graduate of Montana State University and has authored articles for *Decision, Light and Life,* and *Seek* magazines, as well as written a self-help workbook, a teen Bible curriculum, and ten years of Bible studies for the women's program of a church in Kirkland, Washington. She has been an administrative assistant, teacher, trainer, and radio commercial writer. Eileen and her husband, Frank, now live an active "retired" life in Sun City West, Arizona. Eileen combines golf and weaving with her writing to fill her days.

1

"Sh-h-h," Erica warned as Brian's heels clomped across the front porch.

He grinned at her. "They won't eat you alive, you know," he whispered. "You're only twenty-eight minutes late."

"But they'll yell a lot. Especially Mom. You know the lecture. She'll say she needs her rest so she'll be fresh and alert for her job tomorrow, and she can't fall asleep until I'm home. It's even worse when I'm later than I said I'd be, because she says I make her worry."

Brian chuckled. "Forget this quiet creeping," he said. "Maybe you should fling open the door and yell, 'I'm home. You can sleep now.'"

Erica grinned as she visualized her parents' reactions to that. Her brown hair danced on her shoulders as she shook her head. "No," she whispered. "I'll do it my way. Thanks, Brian. I had a great time."

His finger flicked her cheek gently. "See you Monday."

Erica watched him jump soundlessly from the porch and stride across the yards that separated their homes. Quietly she turned the knob and slipped into the house.

Instead of the lecture she had expected, Erica heard voices coming from the den. Her father's low rumble contrasted with her mother's voice, which almost quivered with excitement. "But, Richard, it's the chance of a lifetime. Not just for me, but for the children, too. Think of the cultural enrichment that living in Boston would provide."

Erica sped to the den, shrugging off her coat as she ran.

Her father continued. "A move to Boston is a big decision, Norma. I need time to think about it."

"I don't!" exclaimed Erica. She stood in the doorway, her head thrown back, gold-brown eyes flashing. "I don't want to go to Boston."

Her father looked at his watch. "Are you just getting home, Erica?"

"A little while ago," she brushed off his question impatiently. "What about this move to Boston? When?"

"Your mother has been offered a promotion," her father said, "and it means she has to live in Boston for a year or so. She hasn't accepted yet. We're just talking."

"I don't want to go to Boston," Erica protested. "Not during my last year in high school! I just couldn't miss out on all the senior activities."

Her father got up and came to the doorway where Erica braced herself. His arm dropped around her shoulders and squeezed tight. "I understand, Erica. We haven't made any decisions. We'll have a family meeting tomorrow. Okay?"

Erica nodded. Without saying good-night, she ran downstairs to her corner bedroom. She paced the room, coming to a stop in front of the full-length mirror. She grimaced at her reflection.

Go to Boston now? And miss graduating with my friends? She couldn't stand it. She picked up her brush and stroked fiercely through her hair, bringing out its golden highlights. Tawny brown eyes blazed back at her. Could she influence the decision? She needed to have valid, logical reasons why it would be more advantageous to stay right here in Karston, Washington, than to move to Boston.

Her mind raced furiously as she prepared for bed. Once in a while she jotted a note on the pad on her bedside table as ideas came to her.

———

Late the next afternoon, Erica and her parents waited in the den for Alex, Erica's thirteen-year-old brother. Her parents talked quietly while Erica sat with a book on her lap. A Mozart concerto played softly, touching a corresponding sadness in Erica's heart.

Erica wasn't reading. The music drifted over her while she took a good look at her mother. Her mom could have written the book on dressing for success. Even for a Saturday at home, her trim jeans and tailored shirt looked dressy, better than most of her friends' mothers looked when they went out.

Mrs. Nelson, at thirty-nine, looked like what she was, a successful businesswoman. Though a bit shorter than Erica's own five-foot-eight frame, she was almost as slender. Her short dark brown hair swirled in a sophisticated hairstyle.

She was almost too perfect. Erica felt as though her mother held her at a distance.

Dad was different. Her face softened as she looked at him.

He was in his "standard" dress—Dockers, a plain shirt, and a V-neck sweater. Today's sweater was blue, which matched his eyes. Dad always looked so comfortable, no matter what he wore.

He's successful, too, thought Erica. *But he's successful in life and living, not just business.* Her father owned, published, and edited Karston's weekly newspaper, *The Karston Kerusso.* He didn't make as much money as her mother did, but he was happy and content. Her mother wasn't. Mom was always driving, striving for more.

Erica's thoughts were interrupted as Alex burst into the den, dragging a small spiral notebook from one pocket and a stubby pencil from another. "I'm here. What gives?"

For a moment, only the poignant notes of the concerto answered.

Mr. Nelson rubbed his ear absentmindedly. "We have a major family decision to make." He paused. Erica wondered if he felt as apprehensive as she did.

"What is it, Dad?" Alex's brown eyes sparkled. "Or is it a mystery I have to solve?"

"I'll tell you," Erica burst out. "Mom wants to move us all to Boston!"

"Boston? That's all the way across the United States. Wow!"

Mr. Nelson smiled. "We should all be proud of your mother.

She's been asked to be an executive vice-president."

"All right, Mom!" exclaimed Alex. "You'll be president before long. When do we go?" he asked without a breath.

"I don't want to go at all," Erica said flatly. "I want to stay right here."

"That's what we want to talk about," Mr. Nelson said. "We have to decide what to do. Let's lay out all the facts."

Mrs. Nelson slid her hand through her hair. "Yesterday, our company president asked me if I would consider the promotion." She reached over and took her husband's hand. "They gave me a week to decide. I would have to spend the first year in Boston. After that year or so, I'd move back here to Seattle."

"I suppose it means a big salary increase," Erica said.

"Twenty thousand dollars more," her mother replied. "It's worth the move and worth the extra responsibility."

"What do you want to do, Mom?" asked Alex.

"Oh, I want to go," Mrs. Nelson said. "I'd like the challenge. And I'd like being the first woman at that level of management in our company."

"Dad?"

In spite of her anxiety, Erica grinned at her brother. He often took over running the family meetings. *He must take after Mom*, she thought.

Tension returned as her dad answered. "Well, I see advantages and disadvantages," he said. "There are cultural benefits in Boston that you'll never find here in Karston or even in Seattle—like seeing the Old North Church and all the other sites of our country's early history. There's the Boston Pops Orchestra and a host of other things."

"Great," Alex replied, eyes sparkling.

"Your mother would advance in her career and continue her success," Mr. Nelson went on. "And I might enjoy getting into the hurly-burly of a big-city newspaper again."

"You could even take the year off and write your book," his wife added.

Mr. Nelson nodded. "Yes, that's a possibility."

"What are the disadvantages, Dad?" Erica asked, eager to hear the negative.

"Well, I'd have to sell the newspaper." He hesitated, shooting Erica his gentle smile. "And I know you'd like to graduate with your friends here."

"Absolutely. And that's not all, either." Erica picked up her list and shifted restlessly in her chair. "There are a lot of reasons for not going. I'd be letting down all my classmates. I'm the main reporter for the school paper, vice-president of the National Honor Society, center on the girls' basketball team, and lots of other things."

"I understand these seem important to you now," Mrs. Nelson interjected. "But within five years, they'll have lost all their urgency. Besides, you can become involved in the same activities in a school in Boston."

"Mom! You know I can't," Erica wailed. "It takes a long time for a new kid to be accepted. I wouldn't get into a single activity, and I'd be graduating with a bunch of strangers." She waved her list. "These are important now. And it is now, not five years in the future."

"Is that your major objection?" asked Mr. Nelson.

"For myself. But how about Alex? He's really close to Pete and wouldn't like to break off that friendship. Would you, Alex?"

Alex shrugged. "It's not all that important. I could find new friends."

Erica glared at her brother.

"Oh, I'd miss Pete, of course," he said, "and there is a new mystery we've just gotten into. I'd hate to leave without seeing it through. When would we have to go, Mom?"

"In three to four weeks. By the end of January. Will your mystery be solved by then?"

"Don't know. Just started on it." He looked down at his notebook. "Of course, if Dad sells the paper, it's unimportant," he muttered.

"The paper!" Erica exclaimed. "Dad, you don't want to sell. Besides, it'd probably take forever to find a buyer."

Mr. Nelson smiled sympathetically at Erica. "I do have a potential buyer, you know. Bert Tyson has been after me to sell for several months now."

"But, Dad. You can't sell to him. You've said time and again that you'd shut the paper down before you'd let him get his hands on it." Erica paused for breath.

"I still don't want Tyson to have the paper," said Mr. Nelson, pulling at his earlobe, "but we must consider all the possibilities in order to make a good decision."

"Mom," Erica said. "Why don't you stall them? Put them off until things would work out better?"

Mrs. Nelson shook her head. "I can't."

"Does it have to be Boston?" Erica asked. "Can't you just stay here and do the same work?"

"No. This first year must be in Boston."

"Then maybe it's more important to stay here," Erica persisted. "You like the job you have."

"This is my career, Erica." Mrs. Nelson stood up and began pacing around the room. "Yes, I like my job, but I want to move up, to progress. Can't you understand?"

"Won't it wait until next year, at least until summer?"

"No. The opportunity is now. It may never come again."

"We don't matter at all, do we?"

"Erica!" Mr. Nelson reproved.

"I'm . . . I'm sorry I said that, Mom," Erica apologized. *But I believe it, just the same,* she thought to herself.

"Are there any other arguments, pro or con?" Mr. Nelson asked.

"Yes," said Erica. "How about the house? Even if you can sell the newspaper, we couldn't possibly sell the house in that amount of time."

"My company would buy it. That's part of the deal," said Mrs. Nelson.

"Or, if we're to come back in a year," Mr. Nelson said, "we could rent it while we're gone and have it ready for us when we return."

"What would you do when we came back?" Erica asked. "Your paper will be gone. You know Mr. Tyson would never sell it back to you."

Alex sat quietly scribbling in his notebook. "Why doesn't everyone do what he wants? Then we'd all be happy."

"What do you mean, son?" asked Mr. Nelson.

"Well, Mom wants to go to Boston and be a vice-president. So, she goes to Boston. Dad wants to keep his paper, Erica wants to finish her senior year with her friends, and I'd like to solve my mystery. So, we stay here."

"But that would be breaking up the family," said Mr. Nelson.

Alex shrugged. "Mom will be rolling in dough, so she could fly home a lot, or we could fly to see her."

Mrs. Nelson stopped her nervous pacing. "You know, Richard," she said, "Alex might have something. I could fly home weekends, and I wouldn't miss that much time with you. It's a possibility."

2

The next day Erica and her best friend, Leslie Thomas, sat in the school cafeteria.

"What's wrong, Erica?" Leslie asked.

"We might have to move. To Boston!"

"Move? Boston? When?" Leslie's blue eyes widened in shock at Erica's announcement. "When?" she repeated.

"By the end of the month. If Mom takes the job, and I know she will, she has to be in Boston the first of February."

"That's just three weeks," Leslie wailed. "Are you sure?"

"Not exactly. I'm almost positive Mom will take the job, but Alex suggested that she go by herself and that we wait for her here. I think Mom and Dad are considering that possibility."

Leslie leaned forward, her blond hair falling over her shoulders. "Would your mom really leave?" she asked.

Erica grimaced. "I think Mom would do anything for her career. You know it always comes first with her."

"Yeah, I know," said Leslie. "We have to find a way for you to stay. You can't leave now. How would we get along without you on the paper and the basketball team?"

"Any suggestions?"

"I'll come up with something. I can't let my best friend move off to Boston without some resistance."

Erica laughed. "Good ol' Leslie to the rescue. You've made me feel better already. Keep your fingers crossed that something will happen so I can stay."

"I'll do better than that." Leslie bounced with excitement. "I just got a marvelous idea. We need to talk to my mom."

14

"You think she could talk my mother into feeling like she does about home versus career? No chance."

"But what if Mom would let you live with us if your parents move? At least to the end of the school year. That's only four months."

"Do you think she would?" Erica stopped. "Even so, I doubt if my folks would let me."

"Don't give up before we try. If your parents are considering the possibility of your mom going alone, why wouldn't they consider your staying behind? Walk home with me after school, and we'll ask Mom."

The passing bell rang, and the girls scrambled to pick up their books.

"I guess it's worth a try," Erica agreed. They bused their trays, then parted in the hall.

Erica couldn't concentrate that afternoon. A mixture of feelings struggled within her. Mostly, she felt resentment toward her mother for wanting to take her away.

As she surveyed the familiar classrooms, she looked at the faces of her friends as if they were strangers. She really did love it here.

Even Miss Adams, the hard-nosed English teacher who had made life difficult for generations of seniors, seemed to have softened. Erica saw real concern in Miss Adams' eyes as she helped one of the students struggle through an ill-prepared debate.

Erica's thoughts were still in turmoil as she walked to her locker after school. She was tired of retracing all the possibilities.

"Why so down, Erica? Did you get that chewing out Friday night?" Brian touched her cheek. "Where's that dimple that's supposed to be there on my best girl?" he teased.

Erica smiled in spite of herself. "What are you doing here? College too tough for you?"

Brian moaned dramatically. "Ah, you've forgotten. We have a date for after school, my love. I promised to take you shopping for your father's birthday gift, and here I am."

"Oh, Brian. I did forget. So much has happened, and all bad."

"Doctor Brian to the rescue. Did you really get chewed out Friday night? Can I help?"

"It's worse than that. We might have to move."

"Move?" Brian became serious. "You mean more than just down the street or across town, don't you?"

Erica took a deep breath. "Mom's been offered a position as executive vice-president. The job's in Boston, at least for the first year."

"A year and then you'd be back? That can't be too bad."

"Brian. This year? Now? I'd have to change schools, miss graduating with my class, miss all the senior activities."

"Has she really decided? Is the move final?"

"You know Mom." Erica tried to keep the resentment out of her voice. "Her career always comes first. Can you doubt that she'll take the job?"

"Then all is not final?"

"No, but I'm dead certain, clear down to my toes, that Mom won't pass up this opportunity. Besides advancing her own career, she's striking a blow for all womanhood."

"Don't be bitter. You and I may want to keep all females tied to the kitchen, but there are some who don't."

Erica giggled. "You know I don't mean that. But why does it have to be my mother who's heading the battle lines?"

"Someone has to. Someone's mother. Why not yours? She enjoys it."

"That's the problem. She does enjoy it, more than she cares about us."

"I don't think that's true. If you'll think—"

"Brian, whose side are you on? Do you want me to move away?"

His hand rested on her shoulder. He leaned toward her, his gray eyes probing deep into hers. "Are you encouraging my affection for you, Erica?"

"No," she answered hastily. "I didn't mean that. I . . . just thought you were my friend, and that you'd support me."

Brian's hand tightened on her shoulder. His voice deepened.

"You know I will, always. Even when I think you're too wrought up over something."

When they got to Erica's locker, Leslie was waiting. Erica saw Leslie's eyes light up. "Well, no wonder you were so long in coming. Sir Galahad is slumming."

Brian airily flicked her aside with a sweep of his arm. "Away with you, fair serf. My chariot awaits to take the Grand Erica to the shopping mall."

"You'll have to fight for her," returned Leslie, blue eyes sparkling. Her teeth flashed in a wide grin. "I'm carrying her off to my lair to beseech my mother in her behalf."

Erica laughed at their nonsense. "You two should be on Broadway, not hidden here in Karston. The world is missing some great talent."

Brian swept a deep bow and Leslie matched it with a low curtsy. "We are honored, ma'am," said Brian.

"Indeed," Leslie added.

Erica shook her head at them. "Les, I forgot that I'd asked Brian to take me shopping this afternoon. Do you suppose we could wait until tomorrow to talk to your mom?"

"Is shopping more important than staying in Karston?"

"Of course not. But my dad's birthday is next week, and today is the only day Brian has free. Dad's car is in the garage for repairs, and Mom needs hers for commuting to Seattle. Today is my only chance to pick up Dad's present."

"I guess it'll have to be tomorrow then," Leslie said.

Brian looked triumphant. "Can we give you a lift home?" he asked.

"Sure. I have a load of homework tonight. I thought senior year was supposed to be fun and easy."

"That's a myth to keep you in school that long," Brian teased. "Don't let the underclassmen know."

A little later, they pulled up in front of Leslie's home. "Les," Erica said, "I've been thinking. Perhaps it would be better if you talked to your mother without my being there. Then she wouldn't be on the spot."

"Okay." Leslie slid out of the car. "I'll be my most persuasive self."

"Thanks, Les. I don't know what I'd do without you." Erica almost choked at the realization that she might have to learn to do without Leslie—and without Brian. He had been her shadow since the day her family moved to Karston six years earlier.

"What's that all about? May I ask?" Brian questioned as they headed for the mall.

"I'm not sure it's a valid option," Erica said, "but when I told Leslie about the possibility of our moving, she offered to ask her mom if I could live with them for the rest of the school year."

"Do you think your folks would let you?"

"I don't know, but it can't hurt to ask."

After an hour of wandering through stores, inspecting and rejecting, Erica grabbed Brian's arm. "Brian, I know just the thing!" she exclaimed, pulling him out of the mall back to his car.

"Where now?" he asked.

"Last week, Dad's office chair broke. One of the arms fell off. He tried to glue it back on, but it's awfully wobbly. Let's go to the office supply store. I'll get him a new chair."

"Whoa, girl. Are you sure that's a good idea? What if your folks move to Boston? Will your dad need a new office chair then?"

"I forgot. It might seem like bribing him." Erica's enthusiasm faded. She turned. "Let's go back to the record store. I'll get him a new copy of Tchaikovsky's *Pathetique*. His old one is scratchy."

————

The week inched its way into the past. Yet, at the same time it seemed to fly. When Erica considered that this might be one of her last weeks at Karston High, the hours melted away. The agony of not knowing made time drag. Studying was almost impossible.

The one bright spot came from Leslie. "Mom thinks it might be okay for you to stay," Leslie reported. "She'd want to talk to your mom first, though."

Erica sighed in relief. "Super. Just hold off until I know what Mom and Dad decide."

Alex was in the hall Friday night when Brian stopped to pick up Erica for their date. He jotted something into his notebook and jammed it back into his pocket.

"Are you working out pros and cons about Boston?" Erica asked.

"What?" Alex looked up. A faint frown furrowed his forehead. "Oh, that. Nope. I'm working on something important."

"You mean a possible change in our whole life isn't important?" Erica asked impatiently. She wanted to shake him.

"It's no big deal," Alex said. "Just a different setting. Life would go on as usual."

"C'mon, Erica. We'll be late." Brian held the door open and pulled Erica through. "You should know that Alex isn't excited about a move. He takes everything in stride. You'll have to battle alone."

"Well, not quite," Erica bristled. "Leslie is on my side. Her mother tentatively agreed to let me stay if my folks go to Boston."

"I'm on your side, too, Erica," Brian assured her.

"Thanks, Brian. I'm just hoping something will happen to keep us here."

"You've laid the groundwork. Now, let's see if an evening out can take your mind off it for a while."

Erica nodded, her anger evaporating. "I wish I could forget that just a few words spoken tomorrow or Sunday may change my life forever."

3

$\mathcal{S}$unday evening Mr. Nelson stood at the top of the stairs. "Erica, Alex," he called. "Will you come up for a few minutes?"

"Sure, Dad," Alex responded immediately.

Erica tossed her pencil onto the article she was editing for the school paper and leaped to her feet. Butterflies took flight in her stomach. Decision time. With fingers crossed, she ran upstairs.

She curled into her favorite chair noticing that her father had chosen the same Mozart concerto he had played at the last family meeting. Was Dad playing it because it was Mozart's last? Because it seemed to say farewell? Was it symbolic of the decision that had been reached?

In spite of her anxiety, Erica grinned at Alex and his little notebook and stubby pencil—as if anything said now would be difficult to remember.

Again Alex took charge. "Okay, Dad, I'm ready. Shoot."

"We're ready, too, son." Dad's smile was soft and tender as he and his wife exchanged glances. He squared his shoulders. "We've reached a decision—what we think best, but we're still open to your suggestions."

Mrs. Nelson shifted in the deep leather chair, the icy-blue folds of her satin robe falling gracefully to the floor. "Unless you really object and can offer a better solution, I'm going to accept the position."

Erica gasped, even though she expected the answer. Tucking her right hand down behind her, she crossed all four fingers, waiting for her mother to continue.

"Your father and I have discussed the possibilities and wavered

20

between two. We made lists of advantages and disadvantages of both and tried to forecast the next year with each option."

"Mom, quit stalling and tell us. We're not executives you need to convince. We're your family." Erica crossed her fingers more tightly. "What are we going to do?"

Mrs. Nelson laughed. "I guess you're right." She paused again. Erica felt the tension stretch to breaking. "We've decided that I will go to Boston alone and—"

Erica expelled her breath. She didn't have to move. She could graduate with her friends. She could stay on the basketball team, the paper staff, and all the other things she had dreaded giving up. When her thoughts returned to the conversation, her mother was still talking.

". . . and perhaps Alex will be able to solve his mystery," her mother finished.

"Any questions or discussion?" her father asked.

"Dad, does this mean you'll continue running the paper?" asked Erica.

"Yes. Perhaps I can also work my book into this year, too." He smiled warmly at his wife. "I'll have more time in the evenings than usual."

"When do you leave, Mom?" asked Alex.

"The thirty-first. I can leave here in the morning, get to Boston that afternoon and be ready to work the next day."

"Where will you live?" asked Erica.

"At first, I'll be staying at a very nice hotel near our headquarters. I'll spend some time searching for an apartment the first week or two."

"And, she'll be home each weekend," said Dad. "This will be a year when weekends are unusually special."

"Will Paula still come and clean for us?" asked Erica.

"Yes," said Mrs. Nelson. "In fact, she's agreed to come in every day from one to six rather than just twice a week. She'll do the housekeeping, the laundry, and fix dinner each evening."

"Any other questions?" their father asked.

Erica shook her head, and Alex made a note or two.

"Then," continued Mr. Nelson, "I assume this decision is all right with everyone."

They all nodded agreement.

Erica rose. "Thanks, Mom and Dad. I don't know how much my wanting to stay here to finish high school influenced your decision, but I'm glad we don't have to move."

She could hardly contain her elation as she ran down to the phone in the rec room. She dialed quickly, shifting from foot to foot as she waited for Leslie to answer.

"Les? Oh, Les. We're not moving!"

"Your mom turned down the job?"

"No. But she's going to Boston alone. She'll fly home every weekend. Isn't it great?"

"I'm ecstatic!" Leslie replied.

"Me, too. I have to go now, but I had to tell you the good news."

The week and a half until Mrs. Nelson's departure went by much as usual. Even Mr. Nelson's birthday didn't make much of a ripple. Alex dashed in and out, held low-voiced conferences behind closed doors with Pete, his best friend. He almost wore out his notebook dragging it out, making notes, and tucking it back into his pocket.

Erica worked at *The Karston Kerusso* every afternoon. She covered the subscription desk and also wrote a column on high school news. After work, it was dinner, then back to the high school for basketball practice. On Friday night her dad went to her game, but her mom was busy with preparations for her trip.

Mom seldom makes a game anyway, Erica thought. It probably wouldn't ever be any different.

Erica noticed her father's sadness as his wife prepared to leave. If he thought anyone was watching him, though, he would wholeheartedly enter into the preparations.

Erica kept thinking, *Why can't Mom be different?*

When it was plane time, the four of them sat in a row at the flight gate. Rain poured down outside the huge windows at SeaTac.

Airport. Some of the drops were getting slushy. That meant snow was falling at home in Karston.

Erica examined her mother's reflection in the window. She didn't seem to regret leaving. In fact, her fidgeting fingers, frequent glances at her watch, and constant shifting in her chair told Erica her mother was eager to be on her way.

When the flight was called, they all stood. Mrs. Nelson rumpled Alex's hair and leaned over to kiss him. He allowed a brush on his cheek, then squirmed away, glancing around to see if anyone had seen.

Her mother turned to Erica. Resting her hands on Erica's shoulders, the closest to a hug she ever came to giving, she smiled and said, "Don't be too angry with me, Erica. Someday you'll understand."

Erica felt a peculiar catch in her throat. Her mother could read her better than she thought. She leaned forward and kissed her mother lightly. "We'll be all right. And you'll be home Friday."

Mrs. Nelson turned to her husband. At last, Erica noticed small signs of distress. For just a moment, her mother clung to her father, and a hint of moisture glistened in her eyes.

"It's only a week—a week at a time," she said. "But I'll miss you. I'll miss you terribly."

"And we'll miss you," he said, holding her close. Then, with his arm still around her shoulders, they walked to the gate. "Call us when you get in," Dad reminded her. "It'll all work out, Norma. We'll make it." He hugged her once more and then she was gone, down the long jetway to the plane.

The other three didn't linger at the gate, but hurried back to the parking garage.

"Here, Erica, catch." Car keys jangled as her father tossed them to her.

Erica slid behind the wheel, and Alex climbed into the front seat beside her. Her father leaned back in the rear seat, his hand over his eyes.

"Miss her already, Dad?" Erica asked softly, maneuvering the car through the airport traffic.

He managed a lopsided grin. "Sure do, honey," he said. "I keep trying to tell myself it's just a week at a time, but the year seems to stretch out forever. I'm not very good at deceiving myself."

Resentment twisted inside Erica. "Why did you let her go?"

"I can't stifle her or try to hold her back. She has a right to fulfill her goals, just as I do."

"Even when they conflict with yours?"

"Of course. There's no reason I must always have my way. I wish she weren't so far away for so long, but we'll learn to cope."

"We will, but should we have to? Why couldn't she be different?"

"She wouldn't be your mom then, honey. Or my Norma. We probably wouldn't love her as much if she weren't just as she is."

I'm not so sure, thought Erica. Aloud she said, "I think a woman—a wife—should give her first allegiance to her husband."

"I'm afraid that the women of today would disagree—call you old-fashioned," her father said.

"Maybe. Up to now, even though Mom's been career-oriented, I haven't felt the results of what that can do to families. Maybe I should suggest this as a debate issue or write a column for the school paper."

"Follow it through, Erica. It's a good idea. Make your own decisions. Then live your life according to the things you decide, your own principles. Your mom and I knew when we married that her career would be important to her, and we've allowed for it. It's worked for us."

"I don't think it's all such a big deal," said Alex. "If everyone's doing what he wants most, then what's wrong with it?"

Neither Erica nor her father answered.

That night, Mr. Nelson barbecued steaks, and Erica fixed baked potatoes and a tossed salad. They were quiet during dinner, each aware of the empty chair at the table.

When they finished, Alex said, "That was good, Dad. You can cook as well as Mom any day."

Mr. Nelson smiled. "Only steaks, son. And before long you'd even get tired of them. It's good that Paula will be cooking for us."

He looked at the empty chair and sighed.

Erica reached out and touched his hand. "Even with a good cook in the house, we'll miss Mom. It's going to be a little . . . a little slow around here without her."

Dad caught her hand and squeezed. He put his other arm around Alex and drew him close. "It sure will."

The phone shrilled. Both Alex and Erica dashed to answer it.

With a baseball slide, Alex reached for the receiver and held it to his ear. Erica made a face at him as he gasped, "Nelsons'." After a moment he held the phone to his chest. "For you, Dad," he called. Then in a whisper he said, "It's Mr. Tyson."

Dad took the receiver. "Richard Nelson here." He listened for a minute, then said, "That's right." A longer pause. "No. The one has nothing to do with the other. I'm not interested in selling. I'll continue to edit and publish *The Kerusso*." After a very short pause he said, "I don't think so," and hung up.

"Well?" asked Alex, pencil poised over his notebook. "What did he want?"

"To buy *The Kerusso*. He heard that Norma took the job in Boston and figured I'd want to sell." He paused as though weighing whether or not to continue. "I . . . I think he threatened me."

4

$\mathcal{E}$rica and her father stared at each other.

Alex's face lit up. "Threats? What did he say?"

"He said I was a fool for turning down his generous offers for a worthless, small-town weekly paper, and that I'd be sorry if I didn't think it over and take him up on his current offer."

Erica swallowed hard. The feeling of impending trouble didn't go away. She riveted anxious eyes on her father. "Dad?"

Her father's face relaxed. He shrugged. "He's probably just angry for not getting his way. He's the kind to yell a lot."

"I'm not so sure, Dad," said Alex, fingering his notebook with his stubby, impatient fingers. "I've been hearing things about Mr. Tyson. I've sorta kept my ears open since he's been hounding you about the paper. Don't underestimate him."

In the face of this threat, other things suddenly seemed less important to Erica. "It's not too late to change your mind, Dad. We could still sell the paper and move to Boston."

"No, Erica. This is the time to stand for our principles." He sighed deeply. "I don't know why Tyson wants the paper. It's certainly not a tremendous money-maker, though it's adequate. Maybe we'll find out why."

"Atta boy, Dad," Alex said. "Stay in there and fight. I'll be with you all the way."

"I hope I won't need more than your moral support, son," Mr. Nelson said, roughing Alex's tumbled hair. "But I can use a lot of that in the weeks to come. By the way," he added, "let's not tell Mom about this. We should save her all the worry we can. We'll lick our battles here, while she fights hers in Boston. Okay?"

Alex squared his shoulders, saluting smartly. "Okay, Dad."

"Sure," Erica replied. *But,* she thought, *a wife should be at her husband's side, sharing these burdens, not a continent away.*

There was no further word from Mr. Tyson that week. In fact, they almost forgot about him as they settled into their new routine. Erica got up a half hour earlier each morning and fixed breakfast for the three of them before she got ready for school.

As far as she could tell, life for Alex hadn't changed a bit, but it was different for her. Unconsciously, Erica began mimicking her mother's role with him. "Don't forget your coat this morning, Alex. It may snow again today," or "Have you finished your homework? No TV until it's done."

She continued to work a couple of hours each afternoon at her father's newspaper. From the office, she called home to see if Alex was all right, if he'd gotten home safely, or if he was doing his chores.

Wednesday when she called, Paula answered. "He's been here and gone," she said. "Erica, may I make a suggestion?"

"What, Paula?"

"Ease up with the boy a bit. He's coping well. He'll be all right."

"But he's only thirteen," Erica protested. "He needs a mother's care, and I'm the only one to give it."

"Just relax a bit. Let things settle awhile."

"Maybe you're right. I'll try, but I do worry about him." Erica bit her lip uncertainly as she hung up the phone. Was she over-doing it? Underneath his calm exterior, he must be feeling as lost as she. The responsibility for her brother weighed heavily on Erica's shoulders.

Her concern only grew. When she got home that afternoon, Alex hadn't returned. She grabbed the phone and started to dial Pete's number. Before she could finish, the doorbell rang. Pete stood there with a grubby envelope crushed in one hand.

"Hi, Erica. Is Alex here?"

"No. Isn't he with you?"

"No. We were supposed to meet here, but I gotta run. Mom

needs me for an errand, and I gotta get a message to him. Can I write a note?"

"Sure, come in. Do you know where he is?"

"He was going to check on something at City Hall—maybe the library. He'll probably be here soon, but I can't wait." Pete sounded unconcerned as he pulled a pen from his pocket and smoothed out the envelope. He carefully tore off what looked like a grocery list and stuffed it into his pocket.

He looked around. "It'll take a few minues. Okay if I sit on the step here?"

"Sure. Take your time."

About ten minutes passed before Pete said, "I'm done. Would you see that Alex gets this as soon as he comes in? It's really important."

Erica took the slightly grimy piece of envelope. "I'll give it to him."

"Don't forget," Pete reminded, closing the door behind him.

Erica glanced at the note. Then she looked again. Pete had indeed written something, but it didn't make sense.

The message read, "Gbhlm nvvgh drgs wivbi zg 5:81 gfvhwzb."

Erica smiled. Code. She might have known. Alex had a strong penchant for mystery stories the last couple of years. Even the simplest message was more exciting in code. She relaxed. Alex was just making life more interesting. She even chuckled a bit when she tacked the bit of paper to the bulletin board by the phone.

As she did, she saw a note to herself scrawled on a page from Alex's notebook.

E. Had to check something out at City Hall. Don't worry. Be home for dinner. A.

She crumpled the note. As she did, she noticed Tyson's name. She smoothed out the sheet again. On the flip side she read, "Tyson. Palmer. Bozeman. Some past connection?"

A tiny pucker of worry appeared between her eyes. She pushed back her brown hair, then shrugged. Tossing the note into the wastebasket, she walked into the kitchen.

"Everything okay, Paula?" she asked.

Paula turned from peeling potatoes. "Doing great. Alex left you a note."

"Yes, I saw it. Thanks. Anything I can do to help?"

"No. I'm just finishing. But I'll be shopping tomorrow on my way here. If there's anything you want, you should give me a list now."

"I know I need toothpaste. I'll check to see if there's anything else."

The phone rang. Erica reached to answer it.

"Hi, Erica. Brian. How about going out tomorrow night?"

"Sorry. I have a basketball game. We're playing Everett tomorrow."

"Why don't I come watch? We could go out for a Coke afterward."

"I'd like to, but Mom's coming home for her first weekend, and Dad wants us to be here." Her nose wrinkled. "I guess he thinks we need to rally round and let her know we love her."

"I think I hear a bit of bitterness in your voice, fair maiden. But your father's right. You should be there to give her a boost. I'll bet this week hasn't been easy for her."

"Well, it hasn't been all that easy here, either!"

"All the more reason you should be glad to see her. But we'll talk about that later. I have another plan. How about a concert with me Saturday night? The school music department is putting on a series based on the kind of programs the Boston Pops does."

"Love to. It sounds like fun. But how about you? That's not exactly your kind of music."

"The ads guarantee it's light enough to please the most plebeian tastes. I guess that includes me. I'll pick you up at seven."

"I'll be ready." Erica hung up, feeling a little better. Brian was such a good friend.

Paula sounded happy, too. She was humming a lilting melody as she finished dinner preparations.

"What's that tune, Paula? It's really catchy."

"Just a little chorus I learned at church called 'Bind Us Together in You.'" She hummed a couple more bars, then with a rich alto voice sang, "Lord, we're all so different, yet we're one in You. Bind us together as only You can do. Take all our separate talents and bring them into balance. Bind us together in You. Reach down from heaven above and fill us with Your love. Oh, bind us together in You."

Erica felt a catch in her throat. "That's lovely," she said. *That's what this family needs right now,* she thought. *To be bound together.*

————

The next day Erica was surprisingly eager to see her mother. Yet, she still felt some resentment. As game time approached, Erica dressed in her red and black basketball uniform and stepped onto the court. *Even Dad won't be in the stands tonight,* she thought. Mom's plane would touch down about eight o'clock, and they wouldn't get home until the same time Erica did.

She shrugged and glanced at Nancy. Nancy never had anyone at the games. Her parents were divorced, her father gone. Her mother's long working hours prevented her from getting to the games. Erica knew she shouldn't complain. Her dad was usually there.

Suddenly, Carolyn White's strident voice pierced Erica's thoughts. "Hey, Nelson. Heard your folks broke up, and your mom's gone off to Boston. Didn't expect to see you playing ball tonight."

Erica stiffened. For several months Carolyn had seemed to delight in tormenting her. "My folks did not split up," Erica defended. "Mom's just working in Boston for a while. She's on her way home right now."

"Yeah?" Carolyn slipped her glossy black hair into a ponytail. "That's not what I heard."

Erica's response was cut off by the coach. "Okay, girls, let's go over the game plan one last time."

Carolyn's taunts wouldn't stop running around in Erica's head. Were people really thinking her mom had left her dad? Then another thought, much worse, made her catch her breath. Was it true?

The idea niggled at her during warm-up, and anger began to grow. When the game started, however, she determinedly put it out of her mind. In the excitement of the play, she concentrated solely on winning.

By the end of the third quarter, Karston had a comfortable lead and the coach substituted liberally. "Good game, Erica," Coach said. "I didn't hear your dad in the crowd."

"He couldn't be here tonight. He had to meet Mom's plane."

Sitting on the bench, Carolyn's insinuations again claimed Erica's thoughts. Could they be true?

After the game, she showered and changed as fast as possible, eager to get home to see her parents. Could something be wrong in their relationship? Something she'd not noticed before?

Erica was halfway down the school steps when she heard her name.

"Erica. Wait up. Did you forget me?"

Erica turned. Leslie stood at the door waving her clarinet. "Les. I'm really in a hurry. Mind if I go ahead?"

"I'll be with you in thirty seconds flat," Leslie said. Without waiting for an answer, she disappeared inside the school.

Erica paced the steps. Leslie's thirty seconds seemed like ten minutes, but finally she came flying down the steps, putting her coat on as she ran.

"There, I wasn't too long. What's your hurry?"

The girls started down the walk, away from the others, before Erica responded. "I don't really know. Maybe it was something Carolyn said."

"Oh, Erica. You should know better than to pay any attention to Carolyn. She has a mean tongue, and she's out to cause you trouble."

"I know. I've tried to tell myself that, but somewhere deep inside me I'm scared."

"Scared?" Leslie spluttered. "Erica, that doesn't sound like you. What's up?"

"I . . . I'm afraid that I'll get home and find out Mom didn't come home this weekend"—Erica blurted—"that she's not going to come home."

"That's silly. Of course she'll be there. It's not like your folks got divorced or something."

"In a way, it almost is," Erica confessed. "She's gone. For a whole year her life will be separate from ours."

"But you've never been close to her, Erica. Does it really matter so much?"

"Somehow, it does."

They reached the corner where their ways parted. Leslie put a hand on Erica's shoulder, then hugged her tightly. "It'll be all right. I know it will."

"Thanks, Les. I'll hurry now." As Erica jogged down the street, the chorus she'd heard Paula singing Wednesday ran through her mind. "Bind us together as only You can do."

Light glowed from almost every window. Erica burst into the house, dropped her sports bag and coat in the hall, and pushed open the living room door.

Her mom and dad stood in front of the fireplace, hand in hand. "Oh, Mom! It's good to see you." Erica threw her arms around her mother.

Mrs. Nelson's hands raised to Erica's shoulders, tightening momentarily. "Ooh, you're cold. It's good to see you, too. I'm glad to be home."

"Hi, Dad." Erica looked at her father's sparkling eyes.

He pulled his wife toward him.

"I see you're glad she's home, too," Erica said with relief.

"You bet. This has been one of the longest weeks in history, but it's over. The rest will pass, too."

Erica grinned. Her heart lifted. Everything was okay. She should know better than to let Carolyn White upset her.

———

The next morning, after a late, leisurely breakfast, Erica leaned back in her chair. "I have a date with Brian tonight. We're going to a pops concert at the community college, okay?"

Mrs. Nelson frowned. "Your dad and I are planning to dine with the Overstreets. I thought you might be here with Alex."

"Alex will be all right. I've never had to stay with him before. He can invite Pete over or go to Pete's."

"I don't want him deserted," Mrs. Nelson protested. "Is the concert so important?"

"Is your dinner so important?"

"Erica!" Mr. Nelson stopped their words, but more gently than usual. "Norma, I think we can let things go on as usual. Alex doesn't need a baby-sitter. He can come with us, go to Pete's, or have Pete over, as Erica suggested. It will be all right."

"Maybe we should stay home."

"No. That's not necessary. Relax."

Erica flashed a grateful look at her father and excused herself.

The rest of the day sped by as she busily sorted the contents of a closet, then spent a leisurely afternoon reworking an article for *The Karston Kerusso*. Somehow she felt impelled to avoid her mother.

It was a relief when her parents left for their dinner engagement. "We're off, Erica," her dad called. "We should be home by eleven or eleven-thirty. Midnight at the latest. Will you be in by then?"

"I'm not sure, Dad. I don't know how long the concert will last. Brian and I will probably stop somewhere for a bite to eat."

"Okay. Don't be too late."

Erica's short, pleated skirt and tailored blouse and vest accented her tall, slender figure. She added just a touch of gloss to her lips and was ready.

Just as she and Brian stepped out the door, Alex called out, "Hey, Brian. Can you give me a lift?"

"Sure 'nuff. Where would you like to go?"

"Over to Pete's."

"Let's go."

"I have to get something. Be right back." Alex dashed down the stairs and returned carrying a grocery bag.

"What's in there? Hidden treasure?" Brian teased.

"Naw, just some research material Pete and I have to look over."

By the time Brian and Erica reached the auditorium, the orchestra was tuning up.

"I'd hoped to be here earlier to get good seats," Brian remarked. "Ah, there's a couple. Let's see if they're available." Brian leaned over. "Hey, Mike. Hi. These seats taken?"

"No. A couple just abandoned them. They saw someone they knew over there"—he waved his arm toward the other side of the auditorium —"and went to sit with them."

Brian ushered Erica into the seat beside Mike. "Erica, I'd like you to meet Mike Havig. He's in a couple of my classes. Mike, this is Erica Nelson, my neighbor."

"Hi, Erica."

Erica smiled, then blinked. Blood rushed to her cheeks as she realized she was staring. "Hi, Mike," she managed to say.

5

$\mathcal{E}$rica was so aware of how good-looking Mike was, she had trouble concentrating on the music. His almost black, wavy hair parted neatly on the side. His eyes were a deep, vivid blue set in a well-tanned, rugged face.

Erica pinched herself. Was she dreaming? The music flowed over her. Brian jostled her arm as he shifted in his seat. No, she was wide awake, and she had met the hero of her girlhood dreams. *Is his personality as great as his looks?* she wondered.

The music selection ended and Erica noticed that Mike applauded appreciatively, not just politely like Brian. Hmmm. *Good looks and he likes music,* she thought.

The first piece had been unfamiliar to Erica, but now the orchestra changed tempo. A lively medley of popular favorites filled the room with rhythm and harmony.

The next number was a march. Erica glanced at her program. The concert was called "Looking Toward Spring" and featured Scandinavian composers. She listened to *Alla Marcia* while reading the blurb. "Composed by Sibelius for a pageant in Helsinki, *Alla Marcia* was part of the Karelia Suite, which had been a smashing success."

Erica settled back in her seat and let the lively, exuberant music pulsate around her. It made her heart pound—or was it something other than the music?

At intermission, Mike leaned forward. "Say, isn't this great?"

"Well," hedged Brian.

"Oh, I loved it!" Erica replied. "It's wonderful music. I haven't heard the Scandinavian pieces before."

35

"I know some of them, but not all," Mike said. "I've been eager to hear this concert—something of my cultural heritage."

"You're Scandinavian?" asked Erica, noting his dark hair.

Mike chuckled. "With a name like Havig? Sure am. Three of my grandparents were born in Norway. One of my grandmothers used to sing Norwegian folk tunes and children's songs."

"I'm surprised. That was all pretty good," said Brian with a grin, "but I really liked the stuff in between. That Elton John song was my favorite."

Mike chuckled. "I like those kind of songs, too. They're more today's kind of music."

When the conductor returned, the orchestra began with the "Rigaudon" from Grieg's *Holberg Suite*. The music was light and happy. Erica settled back to enjoy the last half of the concert.

When it ended, Brian helped Erica with her coat, then turned to Mike, "We're going to The Shack. Want to join us?"

Mike looked questioningly at Erica.

She nodded up at him. He towered eight or nine inches over her. "We'd love to have you come along."

In the restaurant, they ordered a shrimp, mushroom, and tomato pizza, with a pitcher of Coke.

Erica started the conversation. "Brian mentioned you were in some of his classes. Are you in the business curriculum, too?"

"No, horticulture."

"How do you overlap classes?"

"Along with growing plants, we need to know how to keep track of what we spend and take in, so we're required to take accounting. That's where I met Brian. And I must say, he's been a real buddy. He's helped me immensely in understanding some of that stuff."

Brian raised his left eyebrow. "Business whiz to the rescue of the guy who grows my food. How could I let him fail? I may not eat."

"There's a difference between my goals as a horticulturist and the farmer who raises your food."

"Yeah, but guys like you start all the home garden veggies that eventually reach my table."

They laughed.

"Brian thinks of his stomach most of the time," Erica teased. "It's a wonder he's not fifty pounds heavier."

"That's easy to explain. I expend a lot of energy running after the lovely Erica. But she's elusive. Can't ever catch her."

Erica blushed. "Actually, he spends most of his time running away. I'm dangerous and he knows it."

"Yeah." Brian wiggled the little finger of his left hand. A white scar ran across it diagonally. "Almost gave up my little finger for Erica one day."

Erica laughed. "It was your own fault. You should have been paying attention to the saw, not Maggie in her short shorts."

"See," said Brian, his left eyebrow raised. "She's not even properly grateful. She just had to have a bird feeder for her backyard. So I obliged. 'Bout cut my finger off. But does she care? Not one whip."

"The way I remember it," said Erica, "I cried all the way to the hospital."

"Short lived. As soon as they told you I wouldn't lose the finger, you forgot all about it."

Erica shrugged. "The excitement was over," she teased. "But enough about your heroics. Mike, are you going into landscaping?"

"I might dabble in that area some, but I'm most interested in the wholesale end of developing and growing plants, with some research thrown in."

The waitress brought their pizza, and Erica noticed that Mike was silent for a moment before taking a wedge and starting to eat. Then the conversation started again.

"Now you know about me," said Mike. "And we both know about Brian. What about you, Erica? Are you going to school?"

"I'm still a senior at Karston High. If all goes well, I'll graduate this spring."

"Listen to the girl. If all goes well. She's honor society all the way, president this year, I hear."

"Vice-president. Leslie is number one."

"Do you plan to go to college?"

"Yes. I haven't decided where yet. Perhaps the university."

"What's your interest?"

"Writing, but probably not journalism. Although I like that, I'm more interested in fiction."

"Her dad runs *The Karston Kerusso*," Brian bragged.

"Really! I've often wondered about that unusual name for a paper."

"My dad's somewhat of an independent scholar," said Erica. "Kerusso is Greek for proclaim or announce. Since that's the function of Dad's paper, he named it *Kerusso*. It goes well with Karston."

After they had finished eating, Brian and Erica parted from Mike in the parking lot. As Brian drove her home, he asked, "Have a good evening?"

"Super. Thanks, Brian. It was a great ending to a not-so-great day."

"Anything wrong?"

"I almost didn't get to go tonight. Mom's been gone only a week, but I see changes already. She thought I should stay home and keep Alex company. Luckily Dad vetoed that."

"I don't understand. Seems to me Alex has stayed at home alone lots of times during the past year or so."

"I know. But suddenly Mom decided we'd be deserting him and didn't want him left alone."

"It turned out all right. Why so down about it?"

"I'm not sure. Partly I'm scared because after just one week I see a change in Mom, and there're fifty-one more weeks to go." She sighed. "Also, it's because Mom expects me to do things that are hers to do. It's not that I don't want to do them. . . ." Erica stopped, grappling for words, then shrugged. "I can't explain. It just all seems wrong somehow."

"I'm sure your mother is trying to do what's best. She's a career woman, and I know that this is important to her. I'm glad for your mother."

"Oh, so am I, in a way. But what about the rest of us?"

"Give it a chance to work itself out, Erica. It's only been a week. You'll see things smooth out."

Brian walked her to the door. He crooked his forefinger under Erica's chin and smiled down at her. "Whenever you need to talk, I'm available."

"I'm not sure you're the best one. Your loyalties seem to be on the other side."

"No, I'm an independent. I'm trying to be impartial and logical, with an eye on both sides." He put up his thumb and squeezed her chin. "Time you went inside, Erica. Don't want you to get chewed out on top of all your other problems."

Erica laughed. "I appreciate your concern. Thanks for trying to make me feel better."

Mrs. Nelson left the next morning, and again the house seemed empty and quiet. Erica spent Sunday afternoon studying.

Before long her father called to her. "Erica, how about helping with dinner?"

"Sure, Dad. Be right up." She finished the notes she was making, closed the book, and stretched. Almost done. She combed her hair, washed, and ran up to the kitchen.

"What are we having?"

"I thought we'd try fried chicken, potatoes and gravy, with a salad. Sound good?"

"Mmm. I'll make the salad."

"Oh no. You don't get off that easy. While I'm frying the chicken, you get to peel the potatoes and prepare a vegetable. Alex can make the salad."

Erica went to work at the sink. Her father started to crack chicken jokes as he put the chicken into the pan.

As corny as the jokes were, Erica couldn't keep herself from laughing.

Alex popped his head into the kitchen. "Sounds like I'm missing out on the fun. What's going on?"

"Dad—" Erica giggled. "Dad's been talking about chickens." She laughed again, wiping tears from her eyes.

"I didn't know chickens could be so funny," Alex remarked.

"And you're missing your opportunity to become a world famous salad chef," Dad added. "But no more. You're on as of now."

"It was a trap," grumbled Alex. "I shoulda known that nothing in the kitchen could be that funny." Reluctantly, he started selecting vegetables from the refrigerator to put into a salad.

Throughout the meal Alex tried to top his dad with hilarious stories. When they finished, Mr. Nelson told them it was time to clean up and finish their homework.

Alex looked at the mess and shuddered. "Aw, Dad. I thought we'd leave the dishes for Paula. She won't care."

"If you shudder at this now, think how much worse it'll look tomorrow afternoon when Paula gets here. Nothing doing," Dad said firmly.

When the kitchen looked presentable again, Alex excused himself to "do some research."

Erica put her arm around her father. "Dad, I have an article almost ready for the school paper," she said. "Would you edit it for any weak spots?"

"Sure. And while I'm doing that, you can read my editorial for this week and see what you think."

Erica and her dad settled in the den, pencils in hand, Chopin etudes playing softly. It wasn't long before Erica gasped, sat up straight, and looked across at her dad. He was making notes in the margins of her article.

Forgetting to edit, Erica read on, eager to see what her father had written. When she came to the end, she sat forward. "Do you intend to print this, Dad? It's really strong."

"I haven't made a final decision yet. I'm sure of my facts, and I think the people need to know what Senator Palmer is leading them into. Voters should have all possible knowledge so they can influence the person elected to represent them."

"Did Mom read this?"

"No, I didn't want to bother her."

"But she usually reads your editorials, particularly the ones that really bite." Erica slammed the papers down on her lap. "Oh, Dad!

She should be here, not off in Boston selfishly doing what she wants, and not thinking of you."

"Is that the way you see it, Erica? I don't. Each one of us is an individual with wants, desires, and goals that need to be satisfied. Your mother is simply finding the fulfillment she deserves."

"But a wife and mother should be home with her family. This is where her priorities should be."

"Not necessarily. You've always perceived her only in the role of mother, in spite of the fact that she's been involved in her career all your life. You need to learn to accept her as an individual, a person in her own right, without tags, without limiting her to a pattern that you want her to follow."

"But she created the role of wife and mother," Erica protested. "She didn't have to. She could have stayed single and been a career woman."

Mr. Nelson smiled. "I'm sure glad she didn't. I would have missed so much—not only having her as my wife, but you as my daughter."

Erica grinned. "I guess I didn't think about that. I wouldn't be here, would I?"

"No, and you wouldn't be learning how to accept people as they are and let them be free to be themselves."

"I'm not sure I'm learning that. I don't think Mom should be gone. And I don't understand. If we're to let people be free to be themselves, how can you write an editorial like this about Senator Palmer?"

"Think, Erica. You know the difference."

Erica frowned. She knew what her father meant, but she still resisted. "The difference, as you see it," she said after a moment, "is that Senator Palmer is in public office. He's responsible to his constituents."

"Of course. What he does in the line of work belongs to the people. By virtue of accepting the position, his time is to be spent in the best efforts of the people, not himself."

"But in a way, isn't it the same with Mom? By virtue of being a wife and mother, her time should belong to her husband and children. She should be responsible to those people, to us."

Her father rubbed his ear. "You do have a point. Have you been researching the topic?"

"Yes, at your suggestion. I'm feeling quite strongly about it. Mom's being gone has made such a difference in only one week." Erica shook her head, brushing away unhappy thoughts. "But we're supposed to be working on the editorial, not my feelings. Are you going to print this?"

"Would you, if you were the publisher?"

Erica took a moment to glance over the typed pages again. "You're sure of the facts?" she asked, looking up.

"Unimpeachable source," her father replied.

"You conclude that if Senator Palmer manages to carry through this measure, it would result in wealth for a few, including himself, and a hardship on the average citizen. Are you sure? The advertising about the measure sounds like it would profit everyone, particularly from this county."

"On the surface, yes. But when you start digging into the thing and following it through logically, it benefits only those who are in certain positions. It'll cost the average taxpayer an increasing amount each year for the next fifteen years. As they pay more, they get less. I'm afraid that Senator Palmer is either less honest than I thought, or naive and uninformed."

"What could happen if you printed this? Could Senator Palmer use it against you some way?"

"I really don't think so. There could be some negative repercussions, but the facts are true. The people need to know." He rubbed his ear again. "It would be foolish of me not to check out the risks of publishing, but it would be cowardly to back off because of them."

Her father reached for the article. Erica saw a new look in his eyes. "You've decided, haven't you?" she asked. "You're going to print it."

"Yes. It'll be on the editorial page this Wednesday. Perhaps this issue will show me how effective *The Kerusso* is."

"I predict that the letter-to-the-editor mailbag will be full and overflowing," said Erica. "This will set them on their ears."

"I hope so. Now, about your article," her father said. "When's your deadline?"

"Thursday at four."

"Good. I have a couple suggestions you might consider to strengthen your second point."

Alex dashed into the room. His hair looked as if he'd been combing it with his fingers. "Erica, I lost some important information from my notebook. Remember that note I wrote you the other day?"

"Yes."

"Was there anything on the back?"

"Yes. Three names and something else. Let's see, Palmer, Tyson, and . . . oh, I don't remember."

Alex groaned. "The third one is the most important. I can't remember it either. What did you do with the note?"

"Threw it in the wastebasket."

Alex sank to the floor, clutching his head. "With important words on the back?"

"I didn't know they were important. I figured you were done with them if you used the paper to write me a note."

"What are you on to, son?" asked Mr. Nelson. "Is there some connection between Tyson and Palmer?"

"That's what I'm checking. The third name was a town in Montana. It's possible they both lived there at the same time."

"Why are you checking?" asked Erica.

"Because Tyson wants to buy *The Kerusso* so much he'd threaten Dad. I've been trying to get a line on him ever since he started bugging Dad. And he's so persistent!"

"Have you found anything yet?" asked Mr. Nelson.

"Nothing ready to report, Dad. And now I have to find the name of that town again. Rats! That'll slow me down."

"Well, you found it once; it shouldn't take much time to look it up again."

"It was harder than you think. But if I have to do it over, I have to."

"It might still be in the wastebasket," suggested Erica. "I threw it in the one in the living room, by the phone."

"I'll check," Alex called over his shoulder as he bounded out of the room.

6

*M*r. Nelson published the editorial on Wednesday.

At *The Kerusso* office that afternoon, phones rang incessantly, people dashed around, and the usual Wednesday calm was completely shattered.

Her dad grinned at her. "People do read editorials," he said. "I was beginning to think I wrote to only a few, but the response so far has been steady."

"Do you want me to answer phones today?" Erica asked.

"For a while at least. Margo roughed out a form to use to see how many people agree and disagree. See her for instructions."

For two hours Erica jotted comments and responded to callers. All were upset, many were incredulous, a few were really angry—some with Senator Palmer, some with *The Kerusso*. When it was time to go home, it was a relief to lock the doors and leave the jangling confusion behind.

"You stirred things up, Dad," Erica commented on the way home. "Did Senator Palmer call?"

"Not yet. I sent him a copy of the editorial Monday. I enclosed our home phone number, so I imagine he'll call me there."

But Senator Palmer didn't call that night or that week. Erica almost forgot about him in the deluge of mail. Friday afternoon, she was sitting at her desk in *The Kerusso* office, categorizing replies, when Alex burst through the door.

"Erica. Have you seen this? Has Dad?" He waved a cardboard placard at her. "I tore this off a power pole. They're everywhere."

She grabbed his arm and snatched the placard, holding it so she could read. She gasped. "Let's show Dad."

Erica laid the poster on her father's desk and leaned over his shoulder to read it again. Alex pushed in on the other side.

RECALL SENATOR PALMER!

What do you know about:
questioning regarding drug trafficking?
his "vacation" home?
and the people who visit him there?
Are you going to let him line his pockets—
at your expense?

RECALL PALMER!

"What a bunch of gibberish!" Mr. Nelson exclaimed. "Where did you get this?"

"They're posted all over town, Dad," reported Alex. "I tore this one off the post outside the office."

"It's full of half-truths and innuendo. If Palmer can find out who did this, he'll have a good case for libel."

"Dad," Erica hesitated. "Dad, what if people blame you for this?"

"Why should they?"

"The editorial."

"How could they relate the two? I wasn't attacking the man. I was pointing out the disadvantages of the bill he is pushing. I didn't even suggest that Palmer is dishonest."

"Erica might be right, Dad," said Alex. "Some people won't know the difference."

"That's possible, son, but there won't be many. I think most of our readers are thinking, reasoning, intelligent people. There's no need to worry. Now, let's get home so Erica can get to her ball game and I can pick up your mother."

Before the game that night, as Erica ran through some warm-up exercises, Carolyn lined up behind her.

"Hey, Nelson."

Erica turned.

"Your dad sure knows how to hit below the belt, doesn't he? I saw the posters he put out today."

"Dad didn't have anything to do with those," Erica snapped. "He doesn't work that way."

"Yeah? Sounds like a follow-up on the editorial if you ask me."

Erica choked back an angry retort. She remembered the remarks Carolyn had made last week and the misery they caused her. She wasn't going to let it happen again. "Think what you like," she shrugged. "Just don't repeat what you don't know is true."

"It's pretty obvious to me," taunted Carolyn.

"Dad said there might be a few really stupid people who would think that," retorted Erica. "I guess you're the first."

———

Late that evening, when she had greeted her mother and answered her Dad's questions about the game, Erica grew serious. "I'm afraid that Alex and I may have been right, Dad," she said. "Carolyn White made some stupid remarks at the game tonight about the posters you printed and put up."

"Carolyn White? Do I know her?" Mr. Nelson asked.

"No. She's definitely not one of my friends. For some reason she's been downright cruel lately."

"What's this about a poster, Richard?" asked Mrs. Nelson.

"Someone is smearing Ralph Palmer. Unfortunately they put up some posters immediately after I'd published an editorial against Palmer's Economy Builder Bill." Mr. Nelson handed his wife the poster Alex had pulled off the power pole.

"And a high school girl said you printed this?" Mom asked after glancing at the poster. She reached for her coffee cup. "It's ridiculous for anyone to think that of you," she said, dropping the poster on the floor.

"I agree."

Mom smiled at Erica. "I don't think you need to worry. Your father has an excellent reputation."

Erica bit back a sharp answer. She was worried. Her mother wasn't here to know the feeling in the air. She didn't seem to care much, either. Why couldn't her mother be like other moms? "I hope you're right," she said tartly. "Good night, Dad, Mom. I'll see you in the morning."

Saturday, Mrs. Nelson spent most of the day working on papers she had carried home in her briefcase. After Erica finished her home chores, she spent the afternoon at *The Kerusso* office categorizing the mail that had arrived in response to the editorial.

No one went out that evening. The family gathered in the den. Mr. Nelson and Alex played chess, Mrs. Nelson continued her office work, and Erica curled in her favorite chair with a book. It was quiet except for an occasional comment from the chess players and the peaceful strains of Mantovani on the stereo.

"That's it for now. I can't do any more until I get back to Boston," Mom said, shuffling her papers together and putting them back into the briefcase. "I'm kind of hungry. How about popcorn and apples?"

"Sounds good," said Alex and Dad together.

"I'll help," Erica offered. She quartered and cored apples and sliced cheese while her mother popped the corn. "Mom, aren't you concerned about that poster at all?"

"What?" she asked absently. "Oh no. I don't think anything will come of it. No one could believe that your father would do that."

"But, Mom, people do think so. Shouldn't we do something?"

"Like what? No," she continued without pausing. "If anything needs to be done, your father is quite capable of doing it himself. Relax, Erica. Don't worry." She smiled and picked up the popcorn, leading the way out of the kitchen.

Erica grimaced behind her mother's back. *You'd never worry, would you?* she thought. *We're not important enough to you. Only your own business is big enough to worry about.*

After the popcorn was gone, Mrs. Nelson sat swinging her foot gently to the music of Haydn and tapping her finger on the arm of her chair. "This is so nice," she said. "I'll miss it next weekend."

Erica glanced up. "What do you mean?"

"Aren't you coming home next week, Mom?" asked Alex.

"No." Mrs. Nelson picked a popcorn husk from her sleeve and dropped it in her bowl. "There are a couple of reasons. First, I'm still at the hotel because I haven't had time to find a more permanent place. I also need to follow up some leads next Saturday, and I have a meeting Friday night."

"But, Mom, you promised you'd be home every week!" Erica protested.

"It wasn't a promise, Erica," explained her father. "That was our plan, but it isn't going to work this week. We'll survive." He smiled at his wife.

"Of course we'll survive. We'll do fine, Mom," said Alex. "Don't worry about us."

"She won't," muttered Erica under her breath, "not about us."

"Did you say something, Erica?" her mother asked.

"No. Just thinking aloud. Will you be home the following weekend?"

Her mother sighed. "As far as I know, but even after just two weeks, I find it's terribly exhausting to spend that many hours in the air. I guess it's the jet lag, and . . . well, I may cut back to every other week."

Erica glanced at her father.

He smiled reassuringly. "We've discussed it, Erica. We'll miss having your mom home each week, but it will be all right."

Erica thought she saw hurt behind her father's smile. She didn't protest any further.

"Could we fly out and see you?" suggested Alex. "That would be great!"

"Maybe," said Mrs. Nelson. "We'll have to choose a good weekend after I find a place to stay."

A phone call interrupted their conversation, and the subject didn't come up again. Mrs. Nelson left Sunday morning.

The next afternoon, Erica dashed to the locker she shared with Leslie. Leslie was already there.

"Hi, Les," Erica said, out of breath. "Throw me my coat, would you? I'm going to be late getting to *The Kerusso*."

Leslie tossed Erica's coat to her. "Erica," she teased, "there's a note taped to the locker door. You must have a new admirer." Leslie reached around the open door, pulled the note free, and handed it to Erica.

"Why would anyone tape a note to the door? Why not just hand it to me?" Erica wondered aloud as she ripped open the envelope. As she scanned the note, her face paled, then flushed in anger. "Look at this," she said, thrusting the note at Leslie. "Who would do such a thing?"

Leslie took the note and read aloud. "It's obvious, after last Wednesday's editorial, that Richard Nelson is responsible for the posters trying to ruin Senator Palmer. It's even worse since Palmer is out of town and can't defend himself. You'd be smart to resign your position on the school paper. We don't want Richard Nelson's daughter on our staff."

Leslie's blue eyes blazed. "That's brutal. And they didn't even sign it. Who would write a note like that?"

"I don't know. But I'd give a lot to find out. Les, what should I do? Would it be better for Dad if I resigned?"

"No—at least I don't think so. Why don't you ask him?"

"I hate to trouble him."

"I think he'd like to know. He might be able to do something about it. And I'm sure he wouldn't want you to resign, would he?"

"I guess not," said Erica. "I'd better scoot. I'm late already."

At *The Kerusso* Erica plunged into her work, catching up on what had been laid aside to handle the mountain of mail. She didn't have time to think about the note until she and her father were driving home.

"Dad," she began. "Something awful happened at school today."

"Someone giving you a bad time?" he asked.

"Yes. I found an anonymous note taped to my locker door this afternoon. It blames you for the posters and suggests I resign from the school paper."

He looked at her sharply. "Do you still have it?"

"Here in my pocket." She pulled out the crumpled paper. "Should I read it?"

"Yes."

Erica spread the paper and read the note to her father. "No signature, of course," she finished.

"No. Anyone who would suggest that you resign because of something I supposedly did is merely being vindictive. They wouldn't sign." Mr. Nelson didn't say anything for a couple blocks. "Is there anyone in school who would want to hurt you?"

"No, unless it's Carolyn White. You remember she made some remarks about your printing those posters. A week or so ago, she also said some terrible things about Mom's leaving Karston."

"Why would she do that?"

"I have no idea. For the last few months, she's been making snide remarks, but I've been trying to ignore her."

"Maybe you should talk to her and find out why she's doing it."

"I can't accuse her of writing the note."

"I don't mean that. Just try to feel her out and see if she's angry with you for some reason."

"Maybe I could have one of my friends do it," suggested Erica.

Her father frowned. "That's the easy way out, but under the circumstances, it might be best."

"Should I resign from the paper?" Erica asked.

"No way. I haven't done anything wrong and neither have you." He grinned at her. "Resigning might even make it look like they're right."

"Then I'll stick it out," Erica determined. She stuffed the note back into her pocket. "I wish I knew who did this, but even more I wish I knew who printed the posters."

"I do, too," said her father. "We'll find out."

"How?"

"Things have a way of surfacing. Unless there was only one very humble person in on the production of the posters, there is at least one too many people to keep the secret forever. Right?"

"You think they'll make a slip and we'll find out?" asked Erica.

"That's just what I mean. And if we don't raise a big fuss, it will probably all blow over."

It was raining when Mr. Nelson pulled into their driveway.

Alex popped his head out the kitchen door and yelled, "Hurry, Erica! Phone!"

7

"*H*i. This is Erica."

"You sound breathless," said a deep, masculine voice she didn't recognize. "Did I call at a bad time?"

"No. We just got home. I dashed in through the rain."

"This is Mike. Mike Havig, remember? We met at the pops concert."

"Of course I do." Erica smiled and her heart began to race. "How are you, Mike?"

"Doing fine. I was wondering if you'd be free to go to a party with me Saturday night—that is, if you're not dating Brian on a steady basis."

"Oh no. I mean yes." Erica laughed and started over. "No, I don't date only Brian. And yes, I'd love to go to the party with you. What kind of party is it?"

"We're planning an old-fashioned hayride. One of the guys' dads has a big wagon he'll pull with a tractor. Afterward we'll meet at the Turners' for hot chili."

"If it rains. . . ?"

"The weatherman is promising nice weather, but if it should rain, we'll spend the evening at the Turners', playing games. It's supposed to be an old-fashioned evening, doing something our parents might have done when they were our age."

"Sounds great."

"Dress warmly, Erica, and I'll pick you up about seven on Saturday. Okay?"

"I'll be ready."

Erica hugged herself and pirouetted through the living room.

52

"I have a date with Mike," she chanted. "I have a date with Mike."

Alex grimaced at his father. "You'd think she never had a date before."

"I haven't. Not with Mike," lilted Erica. "That's special."

"Who's Mike?" asked Mr. Nelson.

"Yeah," echoed Alex. "Who's Mike?"

Erica danced over to her father and grasped his arm. "Oh, Dad. You'll like him. He's the greatest guy I've ever met. He's tall and good-looking. He likes classical music, and he's going to be a horticulturist."

"Where did you meet him?"

"At that pops concert I went to with Brian. Brian knows him. They have some classes together."

"Where do you plan to go?"

"To a hayride party. It's supposed to be old-fashioned fun—doing what you might have done when you were my age."

Mr. Nelson grinned. "If so, I probably shouldn't let you go."

For a moment, Erica was angry, but then she caught the twinkle in her father's eyes. "You weren't so bad. I'd probably be pretty safe doing what you did."

"I'm not confessing to anything, but I'd like to meet him before you go out."

"Sure, Dad."

The next day, Erica could hardly wait for lunch break so she could tell Leslie about her date with Mike. She held her secret until they were alone at a table.

"Les, I'm just bursting. I have the best news."

"Whatever it is, it's sure put a sparkle in your eyes. Did you find out who wrote that note?"

"No. I'd almost forgotten about that. Remember the guy I told you I met a couple of weeks ago with Brian? He asked me out for Saturday night!"

"Saturday night! I thought you'd be going to the school play with Brian. It's almost a tradition that you two see each play together. I don't think you've missed one since you were in junior high."

The sparkle faded from Erica's face. Then she shrugged. "Brian will understand. Perhaps it's time for traditions to be broken."

Leslie's blue eyes blazed. "Sometimes you're really heartless, Erica!" she snapped. "If someone liked me as much as Brian likes you, I'd certainly treat him better."

"But Brian and I are just friends. He's like a brother."

"Brian doesn't feel that way. If he looked at me like he looks at you, I'd be in seventh heaven. I wish he cared enough about me to do the things he does for you." Tears sparkled on Leslie's lashes. "Why do you want to go out with this guy, Mike, when you've got Brian twisted around your finger?"

"Leslie, I never dreamed—" Erica whispered. "Why didn't you tell me?"

"If you paid attention at all, you'd know how I feel about him," Leslie stormed. "Everyone else does, except Brian." Leslie took out a tissue and carefully dabbed away the moisture. "And Brian doesn't know I'm alive."

"I thought I knew you so well, Les. But I guess I don't. Brian sometimes teases about more than liking me, but he really doesn't."

"Yeah?"

Erica couldn't respond. Was she being heartless and unfeeling toward Brian? To her he was just a good friend. Did she rely on him too much?

———

At *The Kerusso,* Erica stepped into her father's office to get her work assignment. The two men who doubled as reporters and ad men sat across from her father. She glanced from one to the other, noting the serious expressions on their faces. "What's wrong, Dad?"

"Have a seat, Erica. We'll be through in a minute."

Erica perched on a stool beside a heavily-laden file cabinet. She doodled idly in the margin of her notebook while she listened.

"Anything else?" her father asked.

The older of the two men spoke. "I had an appointment to interview Al Johnson, head of the city council today," he said. "When I got there, his secretary put me off. She said that Johnson had been called to an emergency meeting."

"That happens," her father interjected. "It may not be related to this other thing."

"Perhaps not," continued the reporter. "But when I tried to reschedule, she became evasive—said she couldn't find a time, that I'd have to call Johnson and make the appointment with him directly."

Mr. Nelson rubbed his ear. "That is unusual," he admitted. "Well, men, do the best you can. I didn't think we'd run into this kind of trouble. We may have to counterattack, but I need time to think first. Let's meet with the rest of the staff Friday morning about ten."

When the two men left the office, Erica stood beside her dad, resting a hand on his shoulder. "Bad news, Dad?" she asked.

"Yes. It seems there are a few people who believe I put out those posters." His hands moved in an unusual helpless gesture. "It's so ridiculous. I didn't think anyone would believe me capable of blackening someone's character."

"What's happened?"

"You heard about Johnson refusing to be interviewed. We also lost a couple of advertisers—the Super Drug and Phillips Variety."

"Super Drug! They've run a quarter page ad every week since you took over the paper, maybe longer."

"But not this week. The ad's been pulled."

"That's not fair. They're condemning you without even a hearing."

"They haven't said they pulled the ads because of the poster or the editorial. They just decided not to advertise with us. That's their privilege."

"But, Dad, it must be connected."

"I have to agree with you, Erica, but I don't quite know what to do yet. I didn't expect this, so I'm not prepared to handle it. Hopefully I'll come up with something by Friday morning."

"What a weekend for Mom not to be coming home," said Erica.

"You need her, Dad. Why don't you tell her about it when she calls tonight and see if she could still come?"

"No, I couldn't do that. Her job is important, too, you know. She needs to be at her meeting." He reached over and squeezed her hand. "Besides, I can fight my own small battles, especially when I know you're behind me."

"But Mom should be, too."

"She is, Erica. Wholeheartedly. I count on that. But what could she do if she were here? Just worry with me, and she can do that in Boston." Mr. Nelson straightened his shoulders and thumped his fist into his other palm. "We're just beginning to fight. And you know what? I think we're going to win."

Erica's spirits lifted. "My orders, Captain?"

Mr. Nelson handed her a sheet with several items typed on it. "There you go."

Erica looked it over. "Humdrum stuff, sir. But I'll handle it." More seriously, she added, "Dad, if there's anything I can do . . ."

That evening, Alex called Erica to the phone. "Boy, you're getting popular. It's Brian. He wants to take you on a date, too."

"Alex! You're not to put my callers through an inquisition. When it comes to my private phone calls, forget you're a reporter, or a sleuth, or whatever."

"Aw, cool down," Alex retorted.

Erica picked up the phone. "Brian? Has Alex been putting you through the third degree?"

"No, we were just chatting. I called to make sure of my date for Saturday night and the new school play."

"Oh, Brian. I'm sorry. I forgot about it, and I told Mike I'd go to a party with him."

"I thought I noticed some chemistry between you two when I introduced you the other night. I'll probably regret that evening as long as I live."

"Next you'll be trying to make me believe your heart is torn in shreds and you'll never recover," Erica teased.

"Of course it is," responded Brian promptly. "We haven't missed opening night of a school play for—well, for a long time."

"You don't have to miss it. Why not ask Les? She'd love to go."

"Les?" Brian sounded startled. "She wouldn't go out with me."

"Oh? Try and see." Erica grinned. "You might be surprised."

———————

Friday afternoon, Erica finished her work at *The Kerusso* and walked into her dad's office ready to head home. "What did you decide at your meeting this morning?"

Mr. Nelson looked up from the papers he was working on. "Our first tactic is research. We're all going to keep our ears and eyes open and do some digging to determine why we're being blamed for the posters. The thing seems to be growing." Mr. Nelson pulled at his ear. "We've had another cancellation."

"I took two or three subscription cancellations today, too," Erica added.

Her dad nodded. "We've got to find out why."

"What can I do?"

"The same thing we're doing. Keep alert. Ask questions of anyone who may approach you about those posters."

"Will do." Erica grinned. "Have you set our super sleuth to work on this problem?"

"Our super sleuth? Oh, you mean Alex. I thought I'd mention it to him tonight. He might have time to take our case."

"More than likely he'll tell you he's been working on it for some time."

hat night when Mr. Nelson brought up the subject, Alex fulfilled Erica's prediction. "Oh, Dad," he said. "I thought you knew I was already working on it. I think Tyson is involved in it somehow. If only I could remember the name of that town in Montana . . . I haven't been able to get it again, but I will."

"What makes you think Tyson has any connection with my losing advertisers and subscribers?" asked Mr. Nelson. "He only wants to buy the paper."

"That's it!" Alex exclaimed. "If all your advertisers and subscribers cancel, you'll lose lots of money and have to sell the paper. He could take it over. I know he's associated with Palmer in some way. He just has to be at the bottom of this."

"But, Alex, he wouldn't send me notes at school," Erica said. "I don't think he even knows I exist."

"Don't bet on it. He probably knows more about our family than we do. He could get someone to print the notes and deliver them."

Erica mulled over Alex's theory at the game that evening and again on Saturday morning. But the urgency of the problem faded as she began to prepare for her date with Mike.

The afternoon had been clear and cold—a rare rainless, sunny day in the Puget Sound area. After sunset, the temperature dropped and a gigantic full moon rose in the cloudless sky.

Erica slipped into thermal underwear, then a pair of jeans. She chose a wool sweater of blue, red, and gray.

Brushing her hair in front of the mirror, she paused and studied herself. Her hair glowed golden brown, almost the same color as her eyes. The red in the sweater reflected in her cheeks.

She ran upstairs and struck a fashion-model pose in front of her father. "How do I look, Dad? All right for the most important date of my life?"

"You look great to me."

At seven, the doorbell rang, and Alex made a dash for the door. "I'll get it," he called. Flinging the door wide, he said, "Are you Mike?"

"Sure am. You must be Alex."

"Yup. C'mon in. Dad and Erica are in the den," he said, leading the way. "Do you play basketball?"

"Not much. I did some in high school before we moved here, but I'm too busy now."

"Here's Mike, Erica. I approve. How about you, Dad?"

Erica's cheeks felt warm. She sent a half-angry, half-amused glare at Alex. "Away with you, urchin. Go find a mystery to solve." She held out her hand to Mike and drew him to her father. "Dad, I'd like you to meet Mike Havig. Mike, this is my dad, Richard Nelson."

"How do you do, sir?"

"Hello, Mike. How are you?" Mr. Nelson's eyes sparkled with approval. "So you're having an old-fashioned hayride tonight."

Erica relaxed. She knew her dad would like Mike.

"Yes. Some of the kids were complaining that we always do the same things, so some of the parents came up with the idea of re-creating their favorite teen activities."

"We used to enjoy hayrides. You'll love it." Mr. Nelson touched Erica's shoulder. "Have a good time, Little One."

"We should be back by midnight, okay?" Mike said.

"Fine. See you later."

Erica shrugged into her parka and picked up her wool cap and gloves. She and Mike jumped off the porch and raced each other to the car. Already the evening was fun, and it had barely begun.

In the car, Erica chatted happily with Mike until they drove up in front of the Karston Community Church. She turned to Mike with a puzzled look on her face. "What are we doing here?"

"This is where the party starts. See, there's the hay wagon in the parking lot. Come in. You can meet some of the others."

Inside the church, Mike guided her into a big room where quite a number of kids milled around. Erica knew some of them. Mike kept his hand on her shoulder as he introduced her to his friends. Erica was thrilled to be with Mike but noticed that several of the kids gave her a rather cool reception when Mike mentioned that her dad owned *The Kerusso*. She hoped the Palmer mess wasn't going to spoil her evening with Mike.

As more and more kids arrived, the volume of laughter and talk increased. Suddenly, a sharp whistle pierced the air. Silence followed.

"Ah, quiet at last," said a deep voice.

Laughter rippled through the room.

One of the young men Erica had met earlier laughed and said, "It's time to get under way. Our mechanical horse has been fueled, and the straw is fluffed and ready. Let's have a word of prayer. Mike, would you lead us?"

They all bowed their heads. Mike's hand dropped from Erica's shoulder. "Lord," he broke the silence, "we've come together this evening to have a good time. Give us safety during our hayride, a lot of fun, and pleasant fellowship. May we honor you in all we do. Thank you, Lord. We pray in Jesus' name. Amen."

Erica had never been with a group of young people who talked to God as if they knew Him. *I didn't know this was some sort of religious thing,* she thought.

But before she had time to worry about it, Mike tugged at her hand. "C'mon, girl. Let's get out there before all the good spots are gone."

They dashed for the door and squeezed through with another couple. Erica bumped the girl's shoulder and looked up to apologize. Her eyes widened. Her heart sank. Carolyn White.

8

Carolyn's icy-blue eyes flickered as her fingers flipped back her inky black hair. "How's the little half-orphan?" she cooed.

Erica didn't answer. She turned and followed Mike out to the hay wagon.

"What was that about?" he asked.

"She thinks my mom's left for good, I guess," said Erica. Then remembering what Mike had said in his prayer, she smothered any unkind words. "Perhaps she feels sorry for me."

"Should she?"

"Of course not. My mom's working in Boston, my dad's satisfied, and I'm here to have a good time. Let's enjoy." Erica's mood couldn't be dampened with Mike next to her in the straw. "Just look at that moon," she said. "And the stars. It's a beautiful night. I think our parents had great ideas about having fun."

"Me, too," said Mike. "See those three stars in a row up there? That's Orion's belt. And that's about all I know."

"Ah, I know more. I can pick out the Big Dipper, and I used to be able to find Pegasus, the flying horse."

A feminine voice from the other side of the wagon chimed in, "Isn't that the Little Dipper and the North Star?"

"Not in the east," came a quick reply. "Must be Venus."

A guitar chord sounded, and someone warmed up a harmonica. They sang some oldies like "Comin' 'Round the Mountain," "The Old Gray Mare," and "Clementine."

Then they tried some rounds like "Row, Row, Row Your Boat" and "Are You Sleeping" but dissolved into laughter when one of the guys kept repeating the first phrase because he couldn't keep his place. It worked fine until the very end, when he forgot to stop.

Finally, the music flowed into songs about God which were unfamiliar to Erica. She listened intently to the upbeat words and pretty melodies, content to be sitting so close to Mike.

The tractor meandered up hill and down, over little-traveled county roads, taking the most roundabout route possible from Karston to the Turner farm.

When they arrived, lights blazed from every window of the house. "It looks so inviting," said Erica, brushing straw from her jeans and jacket.

Mike jumped off the wagon and held up his arms to catch her. "I hope it's as warm in there as it looks," he said.

Mike and Erica crowded into the house with the others. Mrs. Turner, a small, trim woman who didn't look much older than Erica, stood by the door, directing the girls to a room where they could shed their coats and comb their hair.

One of the guys started up the stairs with the girls, but Mrs. Turner caught him. "Not you, Jim," she said. "You know where the boys dump their coats." She laughed.

Erica smiled and followed the other girls into the large room. She pulled off her cap and gloves and tucked them into the spacious pocket of her parka. Tossing it on a bench, she began to look around. A mirror, nearly the length of the room, stretched along one wall. The floor was highly polished wood.

"This is quite a room," she remarked.

"Mrs. Turner is a ballet dancer," explained one of the girls. "This is her exercise room."

"I should have known," said Erica. She moved over to the mirror, then stiffened. Reflected in the mirror, she saw Carolyn walk in, laughing and talking to another girl. Erica did a double take. *Carolyn is quite pretty when she's happy,* she thought. *Why didn't I realize that before?*

Her thoughts flew back over the time she'd known Carolyn. Although they had never really found anything in common, it was only in the last six months that Carolyn had been so mean.

Carolyn stepped up beside her.

With a whole wallful of mirror, why does she have to stand right next to me? Erica wondered. *Especially when she doesn't like me.*

Carolyn ran a comb through her already perfect black hair. Her pale blue eyes, which had sparkled a moment before, were cold and flat when they met Erica's in the mirror. Her smile dissolved into a sneer.

"So, here's the greedy one at a church social," Carolyn jabbed. "Broadening your field?"

"I don't know what you mean," Erica said. She quickly freshened her lipstick and turned to go.

Carolyn reached out and grabbed her arm. Erica glanced down at the beautifully manicured pink nails. They were almost frightening in their length. She tried to shrug off the hand.

"You'd think that one dedicated guy would be enough for any girl, but not you. You have to have them all, don't you?" Carolyn demanded.

Erica's eyes widened in surprise. "I haven't the faintest idea what you're talking about, and I really don't think I care. Let go of me."

Carolyn's hold tightened. "You make other girls awfully unhappy when you steal their boyfriends, but you don't care, do you?"

Angrily, Erica raised her other arm and brought the side of her hand down sharply on Carolyn's wrist.

Carolyn let go and rubbed at the red welt on her wrist.

Erica's voice was cold and low. "I haven't stolen your boyfriend or anyone else's, so just mind your own business and leave me alone." She whirled to leave.

The girl who had come in with Carolyn stood in Erica's way. Her face was flushed, her eyes apologetic. She put a hand on Carolyn's arm. "Carolyn, don't," she said. "Mike isn't my boyfriend. I was only dreaming. He's never asked me out."

The girl appealed to Erica. "Don't pay any attention to Carolyn. She tries too hard to defend me. I've had a crush on Mike forever," she confessed with a smile. "But he only thinks of me as a good sport, a terrific helper, and a great pinch-hit piano player.

And I must admit," she said, her brown eyes twinkling, "that I am all three. Now go ahead with the others and have a good time."

Erica joined the party downstairs, but her confrontation with Carolyn tarnished her fun somewhat. All night, Carolyn's words niggled at the back of Erica's mind. When had she ever taken a boyfriend from anyone?

When they arrived back at the church, the leader gathered the group around the hay wagon. "Join hands," he called.

Erica felt Mike's warm clasp on her right hand. She reached out, enclosing a small hand with her left. She turned and groaned inwardly. Carolyn again!

The group began singing Paula's song, "Lord, we're all so different, yet we're one in You. Bind us together as only You can do."

Erica could sing with them on this one. Yet as she sang, she thought, *I don't want to be bound together with Carolyn. She's malicious and petty. I'd be better off without her in my life.*

After Mike drove Erica home that night, he walked her to the door. "Did you have a good time?" he asked.

"Super. It was a different evening than I've ever spent. The Turners and most of the kids were so friendly and open. I didn't understand everything Mr. Turner talked about, but he was nice."

Mike smiled at her. "You'll learn. Mr. Turner was talking about his Lord. The Lord Jesus Christ. He's my Lord, too." His voice softened. "I'd like to see you make Him yours."

Erica hesitated. No one had ever talked to her like that before. "I . . . I don't know what to say." She smiled up at him. "Thanks for the evening."

Mike swung down off the porch. "I'll be calling you. Save some weekends for me."

Erica let herself into the house, a warm glow snuggling around her heart. Although partially squelched by Carolyn's remarks, that glow had grown all evening. Mike was the boyfriend she'd always dreamed about—except for the religious part.

———

Early the next afternoon, Leslie phoned. "Erica, are you busy?" she asked.

"Not terribly." Erica sensed an urgency in her friend's tone. "I'm studying. Why?"

"I'd like to talk. Can I come over for a while?"

"Sure. Anything up?"

"I'll tell you when I get there."

Before long, Erica was sprawled across her bed, and Leslie slouched in the easy chair with her feet propped on the foot of the bed—a familiar scene for the two girls who had been friends for so many years.

"Well," Erica said. "What gives?"

"Nothing really," Leslie said. "I just wanted to talk. Did you have a good time with Mike last night?"

"Fantastic! But that's not what you really came to talk about, is it?"

"Partly. Tell me about your evening."

Erica eagerly complied, glossing over the religious parts. She wasn't sure enough of her own reaction to share it, even with Leslie. But when Erica mentioned her confrontation with Carolyn, Leslie sat up angrily.

"That's just like her to try to spoil the whole evening for you. I hope you really let her have it."

"I didn't have to. Someone else came to my rescue and diluted Carolyn's venom with some kind words and an apology to me."

As Erica described the rest of the evening, Leslie listened attentively and asked questions or commented at all the right places. Yet Erica sensed Leslie was preoccupied, waiting to talk about the real reason for her visit.

After Erica finished, there was a long silence. Finally Leslie said, "You did it, didn't you?"

"Did what? What are you talking about? You're being as mysterious as Carolyn."

Leslie flushed, but smiled. "Nicer, I hope."

"Of course, silly. What did I do?"

"You talked to Brian about me." Leslie studied her nails as

though their manicure were the most important thing on earth.

"Ah, did you go to the play with him last night?"

"So you did do it!"

"What?"

"You told Brian to ask me out. I don't know whether I'm angry or grateful."

"Angry? Why should you be angry?"

"How would you feel if you couldn't get a date unless your girlfriend told a guy to ask you out? It's rather humiliating, even when you're ecstatic at the thought of going out with him."

"I didn't tell him to ask you out. He was giving me his heart-break routine, and I thought you might give him some comfort."

"I'm not sure that's any better."

"Did you have a good time?"

"Superb." Leslie rolled her blue eyes in exaggerated emphasis. "It was great. Brian finally woke up to the fact that I'm a living, breathing human being and not just an attachment to Erica."

"You were never that," protested Erica.

"No, but Brian thought I was." She giggled. "Anyway, that's over. At least, I think he had as good a time as I did. After the play, we went to The Shack and talked as though we'd never met before." She sighed dramatically. "It was fan-tas-tic!"

Erica jumped off the bed and hugged her friend. "I'm glad. Maybe the four of us can double date one of these weekends."

"I don't know whether I'm ready for that. If you were in the same room, Brian might have a relapse."

"Relapse?"

"Yes. Forget my existence again."

"Don't be silly," Erica chided. It was strange. Even though she was happy for her friend's new sparkle, a sense of sadness edged her feelings. "The truth is," she said, "he'll probably forget about *me*, not you."

Suddenly there was a knock on the bedroom door, and it swung open.

Alex's head appeared through the opening. "I'm going to Pete's for a while. Okay?"

"Where's Dad?"

"He hasn't come back from that interview he went on—the concert pianist, or whoever's performing at the Seattle Center tonight."

"When will you be back?"

"By dinnertime. Pete and I have some planning to do, but we should have our strategy laid out by then."

Alex disappeared, and Leslie stood up. "I guess it's time I was going, too. I still have studying to do."

As Erica walked with her friend to the front door, Leslie slipped into her blue down jacket that brought out the blue in her eyes. "I guess I am more grateful than angry," she said. "Thanks, Erica."

"Don't be silly. He'd have found you all by himself sooner or later."

"I'm glad it's sooner," Leslie said, opening the door. "Oh, it's cold out here. I'm going to run."

Erica smiled after her friend, then closed the door. A sadness lingered. Her feelings about Brian seemed to be changing along with all the other relationships in her life.

Change. Almost overnight, everything was changing—how she felt about her mother, Brian, Alex, Leslie. There was an exciting new relationship with Mike, and then Mr. Turner had talked about a relationship with God, whatever that meant. Some of the changes were good, but she wasn't sure about others. Would she lose Brian as a friend if he fell in love with Leslie? Were other people's relationships changing too? Her father's? Alex's?

What I need is a good book, she thought. *Something to take my mind off myself.* She went into the den to see if her father had any new editions to review.

In the middle of her father's desk lay Valerie Donovan's new book. Miss Donovan was Erica's favorite author of historical romances.

Picking up the book, she noticed an old high school annual open to the senior pictures. A note pad lay to one side. "Dinner with Val. Wednesday, 6:30," it read. Without considering that she might be intruding on her father's privacy, Erica leaned over to study the pictures. One was of Valerie Donovan. And she was beautiful.

9

$\mathcal{E}$rica sank into her father's chair with Valerie Donovan's book clutched in her hand. Carolyn's snide words echoed in the back of her head. *"Your folks broke up and your mom's gone."*

Erica knew it wasn't so, but why would her dad take Miss Donovan out to dinner? He'd never done anything like that before.

Engrossed in her thoughts, she didn't hear her father come in. "I see you've found Valerie's new book," he said.

Erica jumped.

Her dad chuckled. "I hope I get to read it before you whisk it out of here. I want to review it for Wednesday's paper."

Erica dropped the book on the desk as though it burned her hand. She stood up. "I may not read this one. It doesn't look as good as her others."

"I thought the blurb sounded exceptional. I'm dining with her Wednesday night."

"I noticed," Erica said stiffly. "I also see her picture in your old annual. She hasn't changed much since then."

"What's the matter, Erica? I thought she was your favorite author."

"She was, until she made a date to have dinner with my dad."

Mr. Nelson draped his arm around her shoulder. Laughing gently, he said, "Don't be a silly goose. I'm just going to interview her. I'm doing a profile on her and her book for the literary column."

"But you've never taken anyone to dinner before."

"And I'm not this time. She's taking me." He smiled at Erica's frown. "I know. But it's all in the line of business and old friendships. You probably noticed that we graduated from high school together."

"Yes. But that makes it worse—an old girlfriend."

"Nothing of the sort. Even then she passed up the usual high school activities for writing. The only romance she wants in her life is the romance she creates for her books."

A tightness eased from around Erica's heart. "I am being silly, I guess," she confessed, "but with Mom away everything's changing. Did you know that Brian is going out with Leslie?"

"You went out with Mike," her father reminded her. "You've never really wanted Brian as a steady date, anyway."

"That's true. It's just the change. Everything is turned upside down."

"You're in a time of growth, Erica—a time when all young people's lives change drastically. Soon you'll be out of school, and that will be practically the only life you remember. As you grow, things have to change."

A rueful smile crossed her face. "I guess I should welcome it, but it's sort of frightening."

Her father drew her close to him, and she snuggled for a moment against his shoulder.

"Can I go to dinner with you and meet Miss Donovan?"

"Nope!" her father responded immediately. "If you were there, I wouldn't get a question in edgewise, and I wouldn't get my piece for the paper. You get to stay home and make sure Alex behaves."

Erica wrinkled her nose at her father. "An impossible task," she said. "He's at Pete's right now, plotting strategy for something."

Her father grinned.

"Do you think he's on to something, Dad, or is he just having fun?"

"He's at least raising a ruckus," her dad said. "I've had a couple phone calls—people wanting to know the reasons behind the intensive questioning he's been doing."

"Who?"

"Store owners. One was sort of amused, but I think the manager of the Karston Cafe was upset. It seems Alex asked some rather pointed questions about why they withdrew their ad from the paper."

"Did you soothe him?"

"I think so, but he warned me he'd throw Alex out if he came around pestering again."

"Alex must have hit a sore spot. He may be on to something that will resolve this mess about the posters."

"Maybe, but I have to stop him. I don't want advertisers to get angrier because Alex is bugging them. I want to get them back, not alienate them."

"Well, I'll try to keep him in hand tomorrow night while you're getting your story."

"At least it should be a nice safe story—without the repercussions of my now infamous editorial."

"It was a good editorial, Dad," Erica encouraged. "Someone just took advantage of it to blacken Palmer's name at your expense."

"I wish I knew who and why," he said. "I have no leads. It's unbelievable, but I'm depending on my thirteen-year-old son. I really hope whatever he's bulldogging will tell us who's behind those posters." He paused. "But—Alex is probably just having fun."

"The only way he'll turn up anything is if Tyson is really behind it all. I think that's the only avenue he's pursuing."

He smiled. "Let's try to forget it for a while. How about dinner?"

———

Thursday morning Erica and Leslie walked down the hall to their locker. *Leslie is even more sparkly than usual,* Erica thought. *There's a glow about her that's different.*

"What gives?" she asked. "You're acting like the cat who ate the cream, to use one of Dad's favorite expressions."

"I hope you won't be mad," Leslie began uncertainly, "but Brian called me last night. He has tickets to a country music concert next week and asked me if I'd like to go."

"Ugh. Country music. You're not so far gone on Brian that you'd go to a country music concert just to be with him, are you?"

"Well, yes and no," confessed Leslie. "The truth is that I've always liked country music. I was afraid to say so because you're so down on it. But Brian likes it; so now I can admit I do too."

Erica stared at her friend as they stopped at their locker. "Last week I told you I thought I knew you and didn't. Now I'm not sure I know anything about you. Either I've been totally blind or you're changing."

Leslie didn't answer. Erica glanced at her quickly to make sure she hadn't hurt her feelings.

Leslie pulled an envelope off the locker door and handed it to Erica. "It has your name on it."

"Not another one," Erica moaned. Her hand was slow to accept the envelope.

"You can't deal with something until you know what it is— that's one of *my* dad's favorite expressions," said Leslie. "It might not be what you think. It could be an invitation to a party or something."

With an empty feeling in the pit of her stomach, Erica slowly tore open the envelope and unfolded the note. It was typed like the last one, unsigned.

"Well?" prompted Leslie. "What does it say?"

Erica held the note so they could both read.

Saw your father out with another woman last night. She was beautiful. Wouldn't your mother like to hear about that! Maybe I'll send her a note if you don't resign from the paper.
P.S. You might check the gossip column of the *Karston High Views* for all the juicy details.

"Was your father out with someone last night?" asked Leslie.

"It was a business appointment," snapped Erica. "He was interviewing Valerie Donovan for the—"

"Valerie Donovan? Our Valerie Donovan? The one who writes the best books ever?"

"Yes. She has a new book out. Dad is doing a profile about her for this week's paper."

"Wow! How did he meet her?"

"They went to high school together. But, Les, that's not important." She held the note between her fingers as if it were contaminated. "What am I going to do about this?"

"Maybe you can just forget it."

"No." Erica rubbed her ear in unconscious imitation of her father. Suddenly she jerked upright. "I've got to talk to our advisor on the newspaper and make sure this doesn't get into the gossip column. I'll tell her I'm resigning, too."

Leslie stared at her in amazement.

Erica thrust her coat at Leslie and scooped up her books. "See you at noon," she said.

Leslie grabbed her arm. "Wait, Erica. Don't give up without a fight. That's not like you. Let's think about it—do some planning, find some strategy to get back at whoever's doing this."

Erica hesitated. "Maybe you're right. We'll talk about it at lunch, but I've got to stop that gossip column."

At noon, Erica sank into a chair next to Leslie in the cafeteria. "Come up with any fantastic ideas?" she asked.

"No, not yet. Did you scratch the stuff in the gossip column?"

"The advisor had already thrown it out," Erica said with relief. "But she looked at me funny. I tried to tell her there was nothing to it, but my arguments sounded so weak—like my dad needed defending. So I stopped."

Leslie's fingers drummed on the table. In mid-beat, they stopped. "Let's ask Brian. He's been your friend for years, and he knows your dad. He might have some good advice."

Erica wrinkled her nose. "He'd say to tell Dad."

"But if you explain why you don't want to, he might come up with something."

Suddenly a hand dropped on Erica's shoulder. She looked up to see Carolyn's familiar sneer.

"Thought there was nothing wrong between your folks? I hear your dad was out with a beautiful woman last night."

Anger stained Erica's cheeks deep red. "Where did you hear that?" she demanded. "I'd like to know who's starting rumors around here."

"Don't get bent out of shape. After all, they had dinner at the Black Angus. Lots of people saw them."

"Did you write that note?" The words grated from between Erica's clenched teeth.

"What note?" asked Carolyn.

"I think you know what note," said Leslie. "How could you do such a thing?"

"I don't know what you're talking about," Carolyn replied. "But I think you've both flipped out." She turned and swaggered out of the cafeteria.

"She's disgusting," spluttered Leslie. "I'll bet she's the one."

"I don't know," Erica replied. "I watched her eyes when I accused her. They didn't even blink or quiver."

———

After dinner that evening, Erica and her father were working in the den. Erica looked up to see her dad's inquiring gaze on her. She forced a smile.

"Something wrong, Erica? You've been frowning at that same page for the last half hour."

Erica closed the book over her finger. The threatening note was tucked inside, and she'd been going over and over it, trying to find an answer.

Her father's calm, strong face invited her confidence, as it had ever since she could remember. Should she tell him? Her finger felt the edge of the note. It would be so easy to pull it out and let him take the burden.

Alex popped his head through the open door. "Phone for you, Erica. I think it's Mike."

She stood up. "I'll tell you about it later, Dad." Her words floated behind her as she ran for the phone.

"Erica? This is Mike. I hear you have a weighty problem to solve."

"What? Who told you?"

"Brian just called. I think he was trying to ask me to pray about that note you got today, but his tongue got tangled up." Mike chuckled. "Anyway, we decided that if it's okay with you, we'll drop over and see if we can help."

A warm, calming feeling swept over her. "I'd love to have you come. I'll make some popcorn."

"Good. See you in about—oh, half an hour."

Erica returned to the doorway of the den and leaned in. "Mike and Brian are coming over for a while, Dad. I'm going to get ready."

"Fine." Her dad hardly looked up from his work.

Erica mixed a pitcher of orange juice and made the popcorn. Serving her dad and Alex first, she carried the rest down to the rec room. Erica was glad to find logs already laid in the fireplace. She opened the flue, touched a match to the kindling, and stood back to be sure the logs caught fire. Finally, she sprinted up the stairs in time to open the door.

"Leslie! What are you doing here?" she asked. Then Erica saw Brian and Mike. "Come in, everyone."

Leslie slipped out of her coat. "You don't think I'd be left out of this when I started it all, do you?" asked Leslie.

As she and Erica took the guys' coats to the closet, Leslie whispered, "You're not mad that I called Brian, are you? I didn't plan a full-fledged meeting."

"I'll talk to you about that later," Erica threatened playfully. "But right now, I'll take all the help I can get." Walking back to the guys, she said, "I've got popcorn and orange juice downstairs. Go on down and make yourselves comfortable. I'll get a bowl and glass for Les, then I'll join you."

Before she went to the rec room, Erica hurried to her own room and took out the first note, which she had jammed inside her desk drawer.

When Erica returned, the others had already begun eating.

"Okay, show us this note," said Brian with a mouthful of popcorn.

Erica held out the notes. "I thought we might as well talk about both of them," she said. "The first may give some clue to the second."

Brian took them, handing one to Mike. "How do we start? What do you want us to do?"

"I think we should start with prayer," Mike answered. "Then maybe the 'what to do' will be easier to find."

The other three exchanged glances. They had never prayed before discussing a problem. Brian shrugged and Leslie nodded. Erica looked at Mike in wonderment. "It might be a good idea," she said hesitantly. "Would you?"

Mike closed his eyes and bowed his head. "Father, we have a problem. Someone is trying to hurt our friend Erica by sending her distressing notes. We need to know how to handle this situation and the person involved. Give us your wisdom and direction. We know you want to help, and we expect your answer as we talk. Thank you, Lord."

Does God really care about such things? Erica wondered.

Brian cleared his throat. "Now, let's get down to work," he said. "Tell us about the notes, Erica. From the beginning."

10

$\mathcal{E}$rica picked up the fireplace poker and jabbed at a log on the fire.

"I got the first note right after those horrid posters sprang up all over town."

Mike held up the note he had been reading. "This one?"

"Yes. I showed it to Dad. He said to hang in there and keep going. If someone didn't have the courage to sign it, I shouldn't be swayed."

"And the second one?" Brian asked.

"It was taped on our locker this morning. I was ready to resign until Les made me promise to think it over first. I'm still not convinced that I shouldn't."

Mike's black eyebrows drew together in a frown. "You have no idea who might be behind it?" he asked.

"I thought it was Carolyn White until today. Now I'm not sure."

"It's Carolyn," insisted Leslie. "Her innocent air and swagger didn't fool me."

"She's the one who made the crack about a half-orphan." Mike commented.

"Yes. Later on at the Turners', she said some more terrible things." Erica felt her cheeks burn. "She accused me of stealing boyfriends and not caring who I hurt."

Brian spluttered. "She obviously doesn't know you—or else I don't. And I think I know you pretty well."

"Was she more specific?" Mike asked.

Erica hesitated. She had liked the girl who had a crush on Mike,

77

and she didn't want to say anything to embarrass her. "Not really. I didn't know what she was talking about."

Brian scooped up the last of the popcorn. "Why would she write the notes? Does she have something against you?"

"Not that I know of. She could just be making smart remarks. In a way, that's more like her. She's direct and ready to confront, not sneaky."

"She's made other remarks?" Mike asked.

"First she suggested that Mom and Dad had split up, then she accused Dad of publishing the poster. Just today, she gloated about Dad's dating another woman."

"Did you hear yourself, Erica?" Brian asked, enthusiasm lifting his voice. "She verbally attacked you on the same issues as the notes. Could there be a connection?"

"Maybe," Mike said. "But before we get too caught up with who and why, I think the main issue is whether Erica should resign or not."

There was a short silence.

"I think I should," Erica said. "It would be horrible if someone wrote to Mom. Dad would be hurt."

"Who's writing to your mother?" Erica's father stood in the doorway, a fresh bowl of popcorn in his hand. "I think I'd better join this powwow."

A look of relief passed over Brian's face. "I agree, Mr. Nelson. I thought you should be in on it from the first, but Erica didn't want to trouble you."

Mr. Nelson gave Erica a quizzical look. "You didn't want to trouble me with something that could hurt your mother?"

Erica's cheeks felt warm. "When you put it that way, Dad, it sounds ridiculous. I only wanted to spare you hurt."

"You'd better fill me in."

Without speaking, Mike handed Mr. Nelson the notes. After scanning the contents, Erica's father looked grim. "There's a word for this kind of thing. It's called blackmail."

"Dad, I don't mind resigning. I don't want someone to give Mom a wrong impression."

"They can't do that, Erica. Your mother already knows about the dinner with Valerie. I told her about it Sunday night. You definitely should not resign. But I do want to get to the bottom of this."

"How do we go about it, Mr. Nelson?" asked Mike. "How can we track down an anonymous note?"

"If we were in an old mystery story," said Brian, "we'd be able to trace the style of type to a certain typewriter and narrow the field of suspects."

"Which is the whole town of Karston right now," murmured Erica. "Besides, we're not in a mystery, and the notes look like they're computer-generated."

"Maybe we should call in Alex," said Leslie. "He's a super sleuth."

"He's working on this whole mess from another angle," said Mr. Nelson. "He may have more information than we do."

"That wouldn't be hard, would it?" said Leslie. "All we have is two notes that were taped to a locker in a school hallway where hundreds of people pass by every hour."

"Did both notes come the same time of day?" Mike asked.

"No. The first one was there just as I was leaving school. Today, the note had been taped to my locker before I got there."

"You didn't see anyone lurking around?" asked Brian.

"No. No one out of the ordinary. I thought for a while that one red-haired boy was staring, but I'm sure it was my imagination."

"I don't think we can accomplish any more tonight," said Mr. Nelson. "I want to thank all of you for caring."

"That's what friends are for," said Mike. "Come on, Brian, Leslie. I'll drive you home."

"I can walk faster," Brian replied. "Les needs a ride, though."

"Sure," Mike said, standing up to stretch.

Upstairs, Brian helped Leslie into her coat, then he and Mike put theirs on.

"Thanks, Les," whispered Erica. "I appreciate what you did."

Mike paused at the door with Erica while Brian and Leslie chatted on the front steps. "Would you like to go to church with me

Sunday and then come home to meet my folks? They asked me to invite you for dinner."

"I'd like that," Erica smiled. "Thanks, Mike. Good night, Brian. Night, Les." She closed the door.

Her father waited outside the den. "Why the secrecy from me, Erica? I thought we could share with each other."

"It seems silly now, Dad. But this morning I was so upset and confused. All I wanted was to save you from feeling the way I did. I didn't realize it would sound like I didn't trust you."

His big hand grasped her shoulder. "It's okay, Erica girl. I headed us into rough waters when I published that editorial. I wish I'd never heard of Palmer or his Economy Builder Bill."

"You don't mean that, Dad. We'll fight it through. I can take it if you can."

"Good girl."

—————

Mr. Nelson was unusually quiet at dinner the next night.

Alex looked at his father. "Guess you're worried about the paper, huh, Dad? It was pretty thin this week."

"We lost a half dozen more advertisers this issue."

Worry clouded Erica's face. "Are you going to be able to keep it going?" she asked.

"We're still breaking even right now, but if we lose any more, the paper will no longer be in the black." He shook his head. "It's unbelievable. How could such a concerted effort to blackball me stem from a simple, honest, above-board editorial?"

"It wasn't the editorial, Dad," explained Alex. "That just set everything in motion. You laid a trap for yourself."

Erica set her glass on the table. "What do you mean?"

"Simple deduction," he began. The ring of the telephone interrupted his explanation, and Alex bolted from the table.

"Dad, it's for you," he called. Coming back to the table, he said softly, "I think it's Tyson."

"Are you really making some headway in checking out Tyson?" Erica asked Alex while her father talked on the phone.

"I think so. But I don't have any proof. That's what I need to get."

Mr. Nelson returned to the table. "I don't like getting calls like that, Alex," he snapped.

Erica looked up in surprise. Her father's face looked drawn, his lips compressed. *He's really angry,* she thought.

"Wasn't that Tyson, sir?" asked Alex, careful to show respect in light of his father's mood.

"Yes. And he was complaining about you. Are you trying to make life more difficult for me?"

"No, sir."

"Then why have you been bugging Mr. Tyson?"

"I haven't."

"Obviously you have. Otherwise he wouldn't have called to complain that he couldn't make a move without seeing you lurking about."

Alex relaxed and grinned. "Is that all?"

Erica stared at her brother. *He's got more nerve than I do,* she thought. *Dad's really upset.*

"All?"

"Dad!" Alex protested. "If Tyson didn't have something to hide, he wouldn't care or even notice if I follow him around."

"So that's what you've been doing. Why?"

"Why? Because he threatened you. The only way I know to find out what makes him tick is to see what he does, where he goes, who he talks to." He waved a hand airily, then added modestly, "I wasn't sure I was on to anything until this complaint. Now I'll really get on his tail."

Mr. Nelson's face relaxed, and his voice sounded more thoughtful than angry. "I can't let you do that, son," he said.

Erica sighed.

Now Alex was upset. "Please don't make me stop, Dad. How can I discover why Tyson wants to buy you out if I can't pursue any leads?"

"Find a different way to do it rather than following him around every afternoon and weekend," his father instructed. "If you can pursue your hunches without antagonizing everyone in town, you can go ahead. But I don't want any more complaints about your pestering. Do you understand?"

"Okay," Alex grumbled. "You'd think catching Tyson would be more important than a few people upset over nothing."

"It could cost me advertisers, son. I've already lost more than I can afford."

But that week even more advertisers cancelled or refused to buy.

Friday evening when Mrs. Nelson arrived home, the family gathered in the den. Erica brought in fresh apple pie and milk for everyone.

"Just how bad is it, Richard?" Mrs. Nelson asked.

"Bad. There are a few who are sticking loyally—Bud Norris, for one. But then, he's my best friend. I'd expect it of him. All those who have signed contracts are honoring them, but almost all the others have stopped advertising."

"Where does that put the paper financially?" Mrs. Neldon pursued, her fingers thoughtfully pleating her gray skirt.

"We're still paying our way, including staff salaries, except for myself." Mr. Nelson smiled ruefully at his wife. "I'm afraid you're supporting me now."

"Glad to do it," she said offhandedly.

Irritation jangled Erica's nerves. *Mom makes it sound like it isn't important, but it is,* she thought.

"I'm considering selling," her father said.

Erica gasped.

"I talked to Stanley Faas at *The Times* in Seattle. I think he would take me on if I came right out and asked."

"You can't do that!" Alex exclaimed. "You have to stay and fight. You've told me again and again not to be a quitter."

"That's true, son, but I have to support my family. If things continue to get worse, the paper will be losing money and it would be a selfish luxury to keep it."

Erica watched her mother for a reaction.

Mrs. Nelson caught Erica's eye and shrugged. "I think you

should see this through, Richard. It's not like we had to depend on the paper. We could lose money for quite some time before we started hurting."

Mr. Nelson rubbed his ear. "I thought I'd always be able to support my family. I don't like being an expense item rather than an asset."

A warm look passed between her mother and father. Erica was amazed. Maybe her mother loved her father more than she thought.

But her mother's next words sounded clipped and hard. "The money's always ours, Richard. Whether you earn it or I earn it. We decided that a long time ago." She sprang to her feet and paced across the floor. "I'm sure this is only a temporary setback. You'll pull through this."

Erica looked at her father. "Have the men at the paper found out why the advertisers are quitting?" she asked.

"No one is talking. Mostly, they mutter some excuse about the economy."

"A poor economy is no reason to stop advertising," said Mrs. Nelson. "That's the time to pile it on."

"I know. But it gives them an out. They don't have to reveal their real reasons."

"I think I might know why, Dad," Alex said. "Remember when the guy at the Karston Cafe got so mad? I was pretending to do a report for school and asked why he'd stopped advertising. When I countered his excuses, he yelled at me and told me to get out."

"Then he called me and complained," said Mr. Nelson.

"But first, before I left the store, he said to the clerk something about—" He interrupted himself. "Here, I'll tell you exactly." Alex flipped back through the pages of his ever-present notebook. " 'Pressure, always pressure,' the guy said. 'If it doesn't come from one side, it comes from the other. Now a schoolboy's pushing.' "

Dad sighed. "Somebody really wants to ruin me—or the paper," he said. "I didn't realize the tradesmen were under pressure. I assumed they were mad because they thought I had instigated those posters."

"It's a ploy against you, Dad. You can't quit now and let them win. You've got to keep fighting."

"I agree," said Erica. "That's the advice you gave me. You need to take it yourself."

"It seems my whole family is of one mind," her father answered. "I guess I hang in to the bitter end."

"Atta boy, Dad," said Alex. "All we have to prove is who is against us and why."

11

When Mike arrived on Sunday morning, Erica was waiting, dressed in her brown and ivory plaid skirt and matching ivory sweater. She quickly slipped into her raincoat, called goodbye to Alex, and ran through the rain to the car.

Erica wrapped herself in her own thoughts as she and Mike drove toward the church.

"I've got a penny," said Mike. "Would you like to talk about what's causing that frown?"

"What?"

"You know. A penny for your thoughts," Mike explained. "Do you want to talk about it?"

Erica smiled. *He's so thoughtful.* "I'm sorry. I was thinking. Mom left again this morning. Dad's at the airport now. She and Dad decided she should cut down on her trips home—to maybe once a month, if that."

"Any particular reason?"

"Two, I guess," said Erica. "The loss of profit for the paper, and wear and tear on Mom."

"It bothers you?"

"Yes." Erica sighed. "Mom should be home, not clear across the country. Dad needs her, especially right now when things are going wrong. She should be backing him."

"What could she do here that she can't do from Boston?"

"Be here to talk to, to support, to listen. Oh, I don't know how to explain what I'm feeling. We all need her, and she's not here."

"Doesn't she call often?" Mike asked.

"It's not the same," Erica protested. Her fingers toyed with the buttons on her raincoat. "I can't see her eyes or her expression. I feel rushed because of the long-distance expense. She should be here."

"Your father seems to think she's giving all the support she could if she were here. Are you expecting too much of her?"

Erica answered slowly. "I'm expecting her to be a wife and mother. Is that too much? It's not physical things I mean. With Paula to clean and cook, we're well taken care of. But I miss her input into the daily things—matters of taste, style, discipline, things I always took for granted. I'm just now realizing how much a mother is responsible for."

"How about Alex? Does he feel the same?"

"I don't think so. He seems to take it all in stride. I guess he's more self-sufficient than I am."

Erica clasped her hands together tightly. She glanced at Mike. "I hate to admit it, but I thought that as mothers go, mine wasn't too great. She's always been too interested in her career. But I'm learning how much she contributed, despite that career. Dad works hard to keep a warm home feeling in the house, but it lacks a mother, a woman's touch, a mood that only a woman can supply."

"And you don't feel able to fill that void for your father and Alex?"

Erica looked at him gratefully. "You do understand. That's exactly it. I feel inadequate. I'm not ready to take over my mother's role. And," she continued honestly, "sometimes I rebel against being forced into it."

"I know you haven't met my mother yet," Mike said as they pulled into the church parking lot, "but you will today. I think she might be able to help. She's a whiz at sorting out feelings and problems."

Erica doubted she could share her troubles with a stranger but nodded. Mike walked her to the door. They slipped inside and found seats toward the back as the choir filed into the choir loft.

Slowly Erica absorbed the feeling of the church, becoming aware of the joy in the singing. In the praise time, several people thanked the Lord for what He was doing in their lives. Their openness, their willingness to admit weakness and failure, as well as victories and triumphs, impressed her.

A man stood up just a couple rows ahead of them and began to talk. "That's Bud Norris," Erica whispered. "He's a good friend of Dad's."

Mike smiled and squeezed her hand.

Mr. Norris continued. ". . . and there's something I'd like you to pray about. I have a tough decision to make this week. I need your prayer support."

Does he have business problems, too? Erica wondered.

The pastor gave a message from the Sermon on the Mount. "Jesus said that Christians are 'lights in a world of darkness,' " the pastor said.

That captured Erica's imagination. She looked discreetly at the people around her, picturing them as little pools of light rushing about in a dark world.

After the service, most of the congregation stood around the foyer talking and laughing. Erica saw the girl who had calmed Carolyn at the party. The girl smiled and waved.

Erica looked up at Mike. "Who's the girl with brown eyes and hair? I saw her the night of the party, but we weren't introduced."

Mike looked up and waved. "Let's go meet her. She's a great sport and our pinch-hit pianist."

Erica almost giggled. That's what the girl had said Mike thought of her. Mike wedged into a place next to her and touched her arm. She looked up.

"Becky, I'd like you to meet Erica. Erica, this is Becky. She's the best little helper the young people's group could wish or pray for."

Becky's eyes twinkled as they had the night of the party. Her brows lifted as if to say, "Didn't I tell you?"

Erica responded with a warm smile. "Hi, Becky. I'm glad to meet you officially."

Then Mike introduced Erica to others nearby. They talked for a while until Mike put his hand on Erica's shoulder and said, "We'd better be going. Mom will have dinner ready."

"Bye, everyone. Bye, Becky," Erica called as she walked out

with Mike. "Hope to see you again soon."

Mike pulled out of the parking lot and headed for home.

Mike and Erica both started talking at once. They laughed.

"You first," said Mike.

"Becky is such a nice person," said Erica. "I feel drawn to her. She's happy, deep down. She seems so peaceful even when she's laughing and joking. She must have an easy life."

"She has her share of problems," Mike replied. "Her father is dying of cancer, and her mother works full time trying to keep a large family together. Becky has six brothers and sisters. Half are older, half younger."

"Are you sure?" Erica asked, amazed. "How can she be so lighthearted, so . . . so . . . more than happy—joyous?"

"It's because of her faith in Jesus Christ," Mike said. "She's learned to depend on Him more than most of us. That's what gives her that sparkle. She knows the Lord can take care of all her problems."

Erica studied her own hands. "I don't know much about Jesus," she said. "But compared to Becky's, my problems seem pretty small. I'm ashamed of complaining."

Mike reached out and patted her arm. "Don't be. I think God tailors our problems to fit us. He knows just what will draw us closer to Him." Mike pulled into the driveway near on an old-fashioned farmhouse. "Let's talk about it later," he said.

"This looks like the house where my grandmother used to live," Erica observed.

"It's one of the oldest in the area," Mike boasted. "It was built in the mid-1800s. Dad and Mom have had fun remodeling it inside while trying to retain its original outside appearance."

"Is your dad a builder?"

"Aha! That tells me you haven't been to the best dentist in Karston. That's my dad."

Erica laughed. "No wonder you have such beautiful teeth. And I thought it was your brand of toothpaste."

"Not in this house. But come in and meet my folks." Mike grabbed her hand and pulled her up the porch steps.

A delicious aroma drew them to the kitchen. Erica felt an un-accustomed shyness. She hesitated at the kitchen door. Mike's mom was stirring gravy while his dad carved a beef roast.

"Mom, Dad, this is Erica. Erica, my mom and dad."

"I'm glad to meet you, Mrs. Havig, Mr. Havig."

"It's nice to have you with us, Erica. But call us Hank and Ellen. We're informal people," Mr. Havig invited.

Ellen Havig wiped her hands and took both of Erica's hands in hers. Curly gray hair framed Ellen's young, lively face. Her blue eyes smiled at Erica. "We've heard so much about you from Mike. I'm glad I get a chance to meet you."

Erica began to feel more at ease. "Thanks for inviting me. It's nice being here," she said. But the noise of charging footsteps and loud bantering drowned out Erica's voice.

The kitchen door burst open, and two younger versions of Mike catapulted into the room.

A welcoming smile lit Ellen Havig's eyes. A similar gleam soft-ened Mr. Havig's words. "Hey, fellows. We have a guest today. Pre-tend you have some manners."

The two boys came to a halt and stared at Erica. "Oh, Mike. She's prettier than you said," remarked one of them.

"Hold your tongue, fella. You're not supposed to blab all my secrets. Well, Erica," he said with a laugh, "now you know the worst of our family. Meet Wayne and Geoff, my brothers."

Erica tipped her head to one side and returned Wayne's stare. "I think I've seen you in school," she said. "Don't you play J.V. basketball?"

Wayned nodded. "Sure. And you're the star of the girls' team."

"Not the star," Erica laughed. "Just one of the players."

"I'm going to be the star when I get to high school," said Geoff, pretending to dribble across the kitchen floor and hook an imagi-nary ball into a nonexistent basket over the refrigerator.

Mike caught Geoff's arm and ruffled his hair. "Not in our kitchen, you're not." He turned to his mom. "Anything we can do to help?"

"You can carry the food to the table," Ellen responded. She

heaped fluffy white potatoes into a huge serving dish. "If you each take something, we'll be ready to eat."

They all gathered around a table in the Havigs' large dining room, which was decorated in rich, warm autumn colors.

Hank Havig reached out his hands, grasping his wife's on one side and Wayne's on the other. Erica felt her hands taken by Mike and Geoff. When the circle was complete, Hank said, "Shall we pray?"

After a short silence, he began, "Hello, Father. We're thankful for this day, for your love and goodness. We thank you for bringing Erica into our home that we may come to know and love her. We thank you, too, for the food you supply so abundantly. Bless it, we pray. Amen."

A chorus of amens echoed around the table.

"Start whatever's nearest you," Ellen urged. They feasted on tender roast beef, potatoes and gravy, succulent corn on the cob, and a crisp tossed salad.

After a dessert of cherry pie heaped with vanilla ice cream, Mike offered to help his mother with the dishes.

"I think I'd like Erica to help me." Ellen turned to their guest. "If you don't mind my taking you away from Mike," she said, "it would give us a chance to get better acquainted."

"Of course," Erica replied.

"We'll all take our own plates in and the boys will clear the table," said Ellen. "Half the work's done then."

Erica scraped plates and loaded them into the dishwasher while Ellen put away leftovers. They worked in companionable silence until they began washing and drying the pots and pans.

Then Erica spoke. "You're just a homemaker, aren't you, Ellen?" she asked tentatively.

Ellen smiled. "I don't care for the word 'just,' but yes, I'm primarily a homemaker."

"Don't you ever long to have your own career, your own way of saying, 'I'm somebody special'?"

"That's not a problem for me, actually. I know I'm special, that I have worth," Ellen said gently. "First of all, I know because I'm special in God's reckoning. He loves me and cares about me, and I'm assured that I have worth in His eyes."

She handed a large pan to Erica to dry. "Then, I know I'm loved by Hank and the boys," Ellen continued. "They may not always show their appreciation, but in their own ways, I know they care about me. But I also have a career. I earn quite a handsome income selling cosmetics."

Erica finished drying that pan and reached for another. "My mom has my father's complete love and approval," she said. "But I'm not sure she thinks about God much. She doesn't talk about Him. She's mostly interested in her career. Without that, she'd feel worthless."

"Perhaps the difference lies in our attitudes toward God. That's the basis for everything else," Ellen explained. "But that doesn't mean a career is wrong."

"Not even when it takes you away and keeps you from being with your family where you're needed?"

Mrs. Havig looked troubled as she put away the last of the pots and pans. "That doesn't sound like good priorities," she said, "but I don't know enough about the circumstances to give you an opinion. Perhaps—"

Wayne and Geoff burst into the kitchen. "Good!" Geoff exclaimed, surveying the clean kitchen. "We're just in time. Dad and Mike are getting out games. Come and play."

"We wanted to play basketball," added Wayne, "but it's raining too hard. Mike didn't think you'd want to get wet."

"And Mike's right," said Mrs. Havig. "I don't." She slipped her arm around Erica's shoulder. "We'll talk more later," she promised.

The afternoon flew as they played several table games. Finally Hank stood and stretched. "Popcorn, anyone?" he offered.

In the kitchen, they all helped fix popcorn, then gathered before a warm, flickering fireplace to eat.

After a while, Erica glanced at her watch. "Oh, my, it's almost six o'clock. I'd better be getting home."

"Wouldn't you like to go to church with us this evening?" invited Ellen.

"Perhaps I can another time," Erica said. "I think I've deserted Dad and Alex long enough now. I don't want them to think I've forgotten them altogether."

Mike drove Erica home and walked her to the door. "Did you enjoy your day?" he asked.

"Very much," said Erica. "Your family is really special. I love them all, especially your mom."

"She is great. I don't know what we'd do without her," said Mike.

Erica's throat tightened. "I wish my mother were like that."

Mike squeezed her hand, then glanced at his watch. "I'd better be going. How about Friday night? Or do you have a game?"

"No. The season's over. They're getting ready for softball now. I'm not very good with a ball and bat."

"Can we go to a movie, then?"

"Love to."

Erica waved as Mike drove off.

In her room, she sat on the edge of her bed. With elbows propped on her knees, chin resting in her hands, she thought of the differences between her mom and Ellen. Both women were attractive and fashionable, but other than that they were nothing alike. Her own mother was restless, always seeking and pushing. Mrs. Havig was calm, radiating peace and contentment.

Why, even with her career, Mom isn't completely happy, Erica thought with sudden understanding. *It absorbs her, yet it never satisfies. She's always trying to reach a little higher, gain a little more. That's the big difference. Mrs. Havig is a happy woman.*

Does God make the difference? she wondered. Would her mom be content to stay at home if she believed like the Havigs did?

Just then Alex poked his head into her room. "Erica, can I talk to you a minute?" he asked.

"What is it?" she snapped, irritated at the interruption.

"I wondered if you'd make a phone call for me. Nothing much."

"I've got studying to do. Besides, that's the kind of thing Mom should be *here* for."

"All I want you to do is make a simple phone call. Is that too much?"

"Yes." An unreasoning anger rushed through her. "I'm tired of trying to be Mom as well as myself."

"Honestly, Erica!" exclaimed Alex. "You're so wrapped up in your own imaginary problems, you can't see the real ones other people have. If you won't do anything, I'll do it myself."

12

"Alex! Wait!"

The bang of Alex's door slamming echoed through the house.

Erica ran to his room. She hesitated, then raised her hand and knocked. "Alex, I'm sorry. May I come in?"

Silence.

"Please, Alex. I don't mind making a call for you."

Erica started to turn away when she heard a scraping noise, then footsteps. The lock released, and Alex flung open the door. A scowl darkened his face.

"I'm sorry," Erica apologized. "I don't know why I felt so angry. I'd be glad to make that phone call for you."

"No thanks," he replied. "I've already thought up a new plan. I don't need you."

Erica reached out and touched his arm. "Forgive me?"

He looked down at her hand, then up into her eyes. The scowl faded. "Sure." A lopsided grin brightened his face. "My new plan is better anyway."

"Anything I should know about?" Erica asked.

"No. It's just something Pete and I are doing. I couldn't figure out one part and thought you might help. But, as I said, my new plan will work better."

The next day, as Erica worked on an article at the *Kerusso* office, a shadow fell on her desk. She looked up. Bud Norris stood in front of her, a harried expression on his ruddy face.

"Hi," she said. "Can I help you?"

"I wanted to talk with your dad," Mr. Norris said. "He doesn't seem to be around."

"Anything I can do?" Erica asked.

A relieved expression passed over his face. "Yes, you can—"

As Mr. Norris shifted from foot to foot, Erica caught sight of Alex hovering by the half-partition next to her desk. *Pest,* she thought.

"What is it, Mr. Norris?" Erica asked.

His hands clasped and unclasped. He dropped into the chair by her desk and took a deep breath. "I hate to do this, Erica," he said, "but I'm cancelling my advertising."

"Cancelling? You can't. You're Dad's best friend." Alarm deepened her voice. "Mr. Norris, you can't do this to him."

"I don't want to, Erica, but you don't know the pressures I'm under." He leaned forward. "Can't you see? No, of course not."

"Is this the decision you asked for prayer about on Sunday?" Erica snapped. "And is this the way you think it should be made?"

"You were there?"

"Yes, I was visiting with a friend. I felt proud to know you then, but now I don't know."

Mr. Norris ran restless hands through his graying hair. "You don't understand," he mumbled again.

"No, I don't understand. I thought the pastor said that Christians were to be salt—the element that stops corruption. There's certainly corruption around here. Someone's trying to ruin my dad, and instead of helping, you're going to destroy him."

Mr. Norris's anguished brown eyes pleaded with Erica for understanding. "I know. I've been battling this for weeks." He took another deep breath. "I just wanted it settled so the war inside of me would end."

"I don't think it will," Erica pushed. "Not if you turn your back on one of your best friends."

"You win." He straightened, throwing back his shoulders. "I'll try to be salt. I hope I won't regret the consequences."

Erica's spirits lifted. "Thank you, Mr. Norris. You'll be glad you stood by Dad in the long run."

"I hope you're right." His smile wouldn't have won the most radiant smile-of-the-year award, but it held steady while he stood and shook Erica's hand. "If you'll stop by tomorrow afternoon, I'll have my ad copy ready."

"Can I have someone pick it up around ten?"

"Sure." He started to leave, then turned back. Picking up a pen, he flicked the point in and out and twisted it in his big hands. "Uh, I'd just as soon you didn't tell your dad about my attempt to bail out," he said.

"Of course not," Erica agreed.

Mr. Norris put the pen down. "Thanks. For everything."

Alex left his eavesdropping position and dashed after Mr. Norris, weaving among the desks to reach him before he got to the door. Alex pulled his notebook and stubby pencil from his pocket as he ran.

Erica heard him say, "I couldn't help hearing part of what you told Erica, and I . . ." His voice faded.

The two stayed by the front door talking for several minutes while Alex scribbled madly in his notebook. Erica saw the familiar wide grin spread over Alex's face when the door closed behind Mr. Norris. He jumped and clicked his heels, hands thrust above his head in a victory gesture.

"Hey, Erica!" he yelled across the office, "I'm off to Pete's. Important. See you at home."

She nodded and waved as Alex disappeared. *What was that all about?* she wondered.

Erica wanted to ask Alex about it at dinner that night, but since she had promised not to betray Mr. Norris, she decided to wait until later. But when they finished cleaning up after their meal, the doorbell rang. "I'll get it," she called.

Brian leaned lazily against the doorpost. "Got time for a Coke with a friend?" he asked.

"Sure," she said. "Come in while I grab my coat and tell Dad where I'm going."

Erica put her coat on and then went to the den. "Dad, I'm going out for a Coke with Brian. Oh, I almost forgot. Bud Norris wants someone to pick up some special ad copy about ten tomorrow morning."

Mr. Nelson looked up and smiled. "Good old Bud. It's nice to have someone you can depend on."

"You bet," said Erica. "Brian's waiting. I won't be late."

At The Shack, Brian and Erica slipped into their favorite back booth.

"Want anything besides a Coke?" Brian asked.

"No thanks."

Brian ordered for them, then leaned toward Erica. "How are things going? Your mom's been in Boston for a month now, and things seem to be all right."

"That's all you know about it," Erica retorted. "The paper is near failure."

"Because your mother went to Boston?"

"No. Another problem."

"You still consider your mom's tour of duty in Boston a problem?" Brian asked.

"Yes." Erica tossed her head defiantly. "If I were married and my husband's business were struggling, I'd want to be there with him. But not my mom. Her only response is that she's making plenty of money to cover his losses."

"That's *something*," Brian argued. "Your dad might lose the paper if that weren't true."

Erica shook her head angrily. "I know, but I still don't like her attitude. She's so . . . so uncaring about everything except her precious career."

"It's important to her, Erica. She has too much going on for her to sit at home."

"But she has a family she needs to be concerned about. They should have some place in her life."

"What do you want, Erica? To have your mother hanging over you all the time, telling you what to do, what not to do?"

"Of course not, but it would be nice to have her around to confer with and for advice."

"If this were your dad's career, would you feel differently about it?"

Erica paused thoughtfully. "Yes," she said slowly, "I think I would. Dad's moved us several times. Each time he moved, it was a step up for him."

"This is a step up for your mother," Brian reminded her.

"Oh yes. For Mom, but not for the rest of us. I can't explain, but with Dad, each promotion, each opportunity was also, somehow, good for the whole family."

"And your mother's isn't?"

"No. It's only for her. It's *her* career, *her* promotion, *her* needs being met. Dad doesn't have a real wife. Alex and I don't have a real mother either."

"Alex seems perfectly content."

"You're right. He doesn't seem to miss Mom," she admitted. "He's delighted when she comes home or calls, but his life goes on regardless."

"So Alex really isn't hurting." Brian reached out and touched her hand. "I'm not putting you down, Erica. I just want you to think about this objectively."

Tears sparkled on Erica's lashes. She dashed them away with the back of her hand. "To you it'll sound like complaining, but her being gone puts a lot more responsibility on me. If Mom were here, I wouldn't have to worry about Alex and what he's doing. I wouldn't feel like I have to take her place supporting Dad."

Brian's hand reached up and lifted her chin so her eyes met his. "You'd do those things even if she were here."

"Maybe." Erica got a tissue from her purse. "But when I'm around your mom, or Mike's, or Leslie's and see some of the things they do for you, I realize how much I miss."

"Be fair, Erica." Brian grasped both her hands firmly in his. "Your mom never has done those things. You should have accepted that a long time ago."

"I could at least pretend while she was here," Erica said, her voice barely more than a whisper. "Now everyone knows that my mom doesn't care about me." A tear slipped out and slid down her cheek. Furiously, she wiped it away.

"Let's get out of here," said Brian. He paid the bill and led Erica out to his car. "Now," he said, "what's this nonsense about your mother not caring about you?"

"Figure it out for yourself. If Mom really cared, would she take off across the country for a year or more? No. She'd stay with us. The only thing my mother really cares about is her horrid old vice-presidency." Erica burst into tears. She buried her face in Brian's chest. His rough sweater felt scratchy on her cheek.

He patted her awkwardly. "This isn't you, Erica. You're my tough tomboy. Tears aren't your style."

Erica sniffed and sat up. "I'm sorry," she said. "I've soaked your sweater."

"If I'd cut off a finger for you," he teased, "I'll certainly not complain about your shrinking my favorite old wooly."

Erica's face brightened a little. "You're such a good friend," she said.

"I'd like to be more."

"You would? It seems I see Leslie looming on your horizon."

Brian grinned. "You know, I never really noticed her before that night at the play. She's real."

An unknown feeling raced through Erica. She shrugged it off. "Sure she is. That's why she's my best friend."

"Better than me?"

"Well, best girlfriend."

"Storm over?" asked Brian.

"Yes. I'd better get home. I have homework yet to do."

When Brian dropped her off, she leaned over and kissed him on the cheek. "Thanks, Brian. You are the best kind of friend."

He squeezed her hand.

Erica watched him ease his car down the street to his own driveway; then she ran up the porch steps and opened the door.

"Erica?"

"Yes, Dad?" She went into the den.

"You missed a call from your mom. She said to say hi and give you her love." He smiled, his eyes shining from his recent talk with his wife.

Erica stiffened. *I'll bet she sent her love,* she thought. Out loud she said, "I'll talk to her next time. How's she doing?"

"Fine," her father replied. "And I have good news. I'm flying out to spend a weekend with her."

Erica studied her father's radiant face. "When do we go?"

He shook his head. "Not we, just me." His blue eyes deepened to sapphire. "There's a company dinner in a couple of weeks—not next weekend, but the following one."

The strange pain that had raced through her when Brian talked about Leslie struck again. "You'd go off and leave us here?"

"You're big kids. I trust you to handle one weekend without your parents."

Erica forced a smile. "Of course. I guess I just thought we'd all go together to visit Mom in Boston. But I'm glad you're able to go. Will the paper be all right?"

Her father shrugged. "Things are so slow now, I could be gone a week and not be missed. The staff can handle anything that comes up."

It was true. Throughout that week, very little happened at *The Kerusso*. Her dad filled the pages emptied of advertising with additional state, national, and international news that he ordinarily used sparingly. He had always said that type of news people could get from the dailies.

Wednesday evening while Erica was home alone, she was surprised to get a call from her mother. "Dad's not here, Mom. He and Alex went to something at school."

"Oh, well. Just tell him I called and give my love to Alex," Mom said.

"Sure."

"How's everything with you?"

"Do you really want to know?" Bitterness tinged Erica's words.

"Erica. Of course I do. Is something wrong?"

"Everything. You should be here."

"You know I can't be there. Is something specifically wrong?"

Erica remembered her dad's injunctions not to worry her mother. "I just wish you cared about us," she muttered.

"I do. You should know that. That's why I'm here in Boston."

"No, it isn't. You're there because you don't care, because all you want is your career. You want to be there."

"That's enough, Erica. You know that isn't true. Success takes commitment, and success in my job is important to all of us."

"Well, it's certainly most important to you. Why did you bother to get married and have children? You never really wanted any of us."

"Eri—"

Erica slammed the receiver back on the hook. Tears of frustration and rejection streamed down her cheeks. *Wait until Mom tells Dad,* she thought. *He'll be furious.* She cried even harder.

By Friday Erica felt better. Evidently her mom wasn't going to tell her father.

Erica spent extra time dressing for her date with Mike that evening, trying a new style for her hair and a different shade of lipstick. After an approving glance in the mirror at her navy plaid skirt and an extra-feminine satin blouse, she ran up the stairs to find Mike and Alex deep in conversation.

"Hi. Sorry I'm late," she said. "Is Alex keeping you entertained?"

"Sure is." While Mike helped her with her coat, he called to Alex. "See you tomorrow about three."

"You're doing something with Alex tomorrow?" Erica asked on the way to the car.

"Yes. He's concocted a plan he thinks I can help him with. I told him I'd be glad to help, so we're going to talk about it tomorrow."

In a short while they were seated in the theater. They smiled at each other. "Oh," said Mike. "Before I forget, Mom wants me to ask if you'd come visit tomorrow. She said something about an unfinished discussion."

Our unfinished discussion about women's roles, Erica remembered. She nodded. Hope flickered deep inside. Perhaps Ellen Havig could help her sort out her tangled thoughts, her weary emotions.

She looked up at Mike. "Tell her I'll be there—about two o'clock."

13

$\mathcal{E}$rica stopped the car, set the brake, and jumped out. She ran up the steps and touched the doorbell.

Tugging at a strand of shiny brown hair, she waited, nervousness now temporarily dimming the eagerness with which she had started for the Havig farm.

The door opened wide. Mrs. Havig greeted her with a warm smile. "Come in, Erica," she invited. "Let's go into the kitchen. I'm baking cookies."

"Mmm. That's what smells so good," said Erica. "Can I help?"

"Just sit and talk with me. I'm almost finished." Ellen rinsed out the baking utensils and stacked them. "I'll wash those later."

"I could help with them now," Erica offered.

"I have a better idea," said Ellen. "How about a fresh cookie and a glass of milk?"

"Sounds good."

Setting a heaping plate of chocolate chip and oatmeal cookies on the table, Mrs. Havig filled glasses with rich, foamy milk. "The best part of baking is getting to sample the goods," she said, sitting down opposite Erica. "The oatmeal have butterscotch chips. They're Mike's favorites."

Erica bit into an oatmeal cookie. "They're as delicious as they smell. No wonder Mike likes them."

"Thank you," Ellen smiled.

For a time, their talk was general. Then Ellen said, "We were in the middle of an important discussion Sunday, and I thought you might want to finish it."

Erica swallowed the last of her milk. "You were telling me that

102

you enjoyed being a homemaker—that God made you content."

"That's true. And I have my cosmetics business besides. I enjoy helping women look their best."

"But you don't make your career more important than your family."

"No. It's only part time. But, Erica, God has different plans for each of us. He always treats us as individuals."

"Then you think that my mother's career is all right, that she's doing what's best?"

"I can't judge your mother. I don't know all the circumstances. And I'm not wise enough to decide what another person should do with her life—other than give it to Jesus."

Erica was about to take another bite of cookie but stopped. "What do you mean?"

Ellen poured them each another glass of milk. "The most important thing people can do is make Jesus their Savior and Lord. God wants that for everyone. Beyond that I don't know God's plans for someone else."

Erica sighed. "If I were a wife and mother, I'd put my family first, not a career."

"But God didn't make you exactly like your mother. Her skills, abilities, and strengths are undoubtedly not the same as yours."

Ellen got up and pulled the last pan of cookies from the oven. She slid the cookies onto a cooling rack and set the pan to soak. "And," she continued, "knowing Jesus as your Savior makes a difference in how you live your life."

"I don't understand."

"Well, the Bible says that sin separates people from God," Ellen explained, "so God devised a way to bring us back to Him. Jesus paid for our sins when He died, and God says that anyone who believes that can become God's child."

"I believe that," said Erica. "I think my parents do too, although we never talk about it. But they're not like you."

"Believing it is true and actually accepting it for your own life are not the same, Erica. Have you ever invited Jesus into your life?" Ellen asked gently.

"Not really, I guess." Erica paused. "If my mother invited Jesus into her life, would she change?"

"I'm sure she would," Ellen replied, "though perhaps not the way you want. Many of us take a long time to learn. But your own decision is more important than what may happen in your mother's life."

Erica thought for a moment. "Would that straighten out all the things going wrong in my life, like Mom leaving and the paper failing?"

"Yes and no," Ellen replied. "God doesn't offer instant solutions to every problem. Troubles may even increase. But He does promise us peace in the middle of troubles."

Ellen squeezed Erica's hand tightly. "With the peace comes strength and wisdom for handling our problems, as long as we keep taking them to Jesus."

"I'd like that," admitted Erica. "I'm tired of trying to work out things for myself."

Happily, Ellen helped Erica pray a simple prayer, admitting her need for God and inviting the Lord Jesus Christ into her life. Afterward, the two looked up at each other and smiled warmly.

Ellen's eyes glistened. "Welcome into God's family, Erica," she said.

"Thank you, Ellen. But what now?"

"Well, if you like, I can teach you more about living the Christian life."

"Oh, that would be wonderful."

"If you could come here each Saturday afternoon, we could study the Bible together," Ellen offered.

"I think I could. There may be a weekend or two when Mom's home that I would have to miss, but I'm sure it wouldn't be often. I'm just so excited about all this, I wish we didn't have to wait until next week."

"You don't have to," Ellen said. She explained to Erica how to have a "quiet time" with the Lord each day, praying and reading her Bible, making notes about specific things that are meaningful to her, personally.

"Do you have a Bible of your own?" Ellen asked.

"No, but I'm sure there's one in Dad's library," Erica replied.

"Why don't you let me get you one so you can mark in it, underline, and date special passages."

"Oh no," Erica said. "I'll get one." She shrugged with a funny little grimace. "One of the advantages of having a mother who's vice-president of her company is having enough money to get the things we want. I'll pick one up on the way home today," she promised. "Do I just start reading at the beginning?"

"During this first week, why don't you begin in the New Testament book of John, keeping a journal of your thoughts as you read," Ellen suggested.

"I already keep a journal for writing," Erica said. "Maybe I could combine the two."

"Excellent," Ellen encouraged. "Now, Erica, be sure to tell the first person you see about your decision to follow Christ."

"I will, I promise." Erica looked at her watch. "Oh, if I'm going by the bookstore to pick up a Bible, I'd better go." She stood, then impulsively leaned over and kissed Ellen's cheek. "Thanks for today. I'm eager to get started."

Ellen got Erica's coat for her. "We'll see you tomorrow at church?"

"I'll try," said Erica. "I'm not sure what Dad is planning."

Ellen's eyes twinkled. "I'm sure Mike could be persuaded to pick you up if you'd like."

A light flush crept into Erica's cheeks, but her eyes sparkled. "Of course, I'd like that best." The pink in her cheeks deepened. "Your son is a very nice person."

"And here he comes now!" exclaimed Ellen, "just in time."

As Mike came through the front door, his face lit up. "Hi, you two," he called. "What have you been up to?"

"Woman talk," replied his mother. "And Erica would like to come to church tomorrow, too. Could you pick her up?"

"Of course. Same time as last week?" he asked.

Erica nodded. "I'll be ready. And now I'd better dash. Thanks again." She ran to her car and started the engine, waving to Mike and his mother as she drove off.

Erica spent some time selecting her new Bible. She was surprised at the variety available but finally chose a study edition bound in beautiful burgundy leather.

Driving home, a commotion on the sidewalk caught Erica's eye. Leslie, waving wildly with one hand, clutched numerous packages with the other.

Checking her rearview mirror, Erica eased over to the curb. Leslie hurried over to the car, opened the back door, and dumped her packages onto the backseat.

Sliding in beside Erica, Leslie slumped down with a sigh. "Boy, am I glad you saw me. I was afraid I was going to have to carry that stuff all the way home."

Erica laughed. "What did you do, buy out the store?"

Leslie gave a guilty little gasp. "Dad's going to think so. But Mom told me I could get a new outfit and the materials I need for art class. That's the heavy stuff."

Talk drifted to school activities as Erica drove toward Leslie's place. She pulled up in front of the house.

Leslie tried to keep her tone casual. "Has Brian invited you to Karlotolo yet?"

"No," replied Erica. "I don't expect him to. Why?"

"Oh, just because he's taken you the last couple of years."

Erica glanced at her friend. "Ah. I should have known. Don't give up. The Karston Founder's Festival is still six weeks away."

"Has Mike asked you?"

"Not yet. He may not even know about the events of the festival."

"Do you want me to drop a hint?" Leslie asked, her eyes glinting.

"Absolutely not!" Erica noticed the expression on her friend's face and relaxed. "I'll take my own advice and wait."

Leslie jumped out of the car, gathered up her packages, and leaned down to say goodbye. "Thanks, Erica. See you tomorrow?"

"I'm not sure, Les. Mike is picking me up for church. I have some studying in the afternoon. Probably Monday."

"Okay, bye."

Erica pulled away from the curb. *Oh no,* she thought. *I forgot to tell Leslie about Jesus in my life. And I promised. Now what?*

Erica frowned. The next person she'd see would be her father. Unexpected reluctance tugged at her. Would he understand? Would he think she had gone overboard? The more Erica thought about it, the less she wanted to say anything. They had always been close. She didn't want to jeopardize that relationship, especially with her mother gone.

She pulled the car into the garage and reached for the bag that contained her new Bible. Somehow the thrill of selecting her Bible had faded. She tucked the bag under her arm and entered the house.

"Hi, Dad. I'm home," she called.

"I'm in the kitchen, Erica. Have a good day?"

"Great. I'll be up in a minute." Erica ran down to her room and put her Bible, still unwrapped, on her desk. Quickly changing into jeans and a sweat shirt, she raced upstairs.

Throughout the evening, Erica studied her father. Would he accept what she'd done? Several times she almost told him. But she was afraid—afraid he wouldn't understand. She couldn't bear his rejection. She knew he wouldn't laugh, but. . . . She didn't tell him.

The following morning on the way to church, Erica rode quietly. Mike broke the silence. "Mom said you had something to tell me, but she wouldn't give me a clue. She just said I'd be glad."

For an instant Erica looked puzzled. Then she smiled. "She didn't tell you anything about our talk yesterday?"

"No. When Mom's in her mysterious mood, forget it."

Erica hesitated, partly to tease, but partly because she remembered how she had been afraid to tell her dad. She wondered why telling Mike was hard.

"Well?" Mike pried. "Are you going to tell me, or do I have to hire Alex to find out?"

"Speaking of Alex," Erica began.

"Oh no you don't," Mike protested. "Back to the news you have to tell. We'll talk about Alex later."

"Okay, okay, I'll tell all," she said. Erica sobered, but joy shone from her eyes. "Yesterday, your mother showed me how to be a real Christian. I invited Jesus into my life."

"Yah-hoo!" Mike yelled like a cowboy at the rodeo. He pulled over to the curb and stopped. "Really, Erica?"

"I thought you'd be glad," Erica said, "but I didn't expect that reaction."

"I've been praying for this since I first met you that night at the pops concert," Mike said. "I just didn't expect God to answer so soon." He reached for her hands and pulled her gently to him. As she looked up into his eyes, he leaned toward her and kissed her gently on the forehead. "Now, if we don't get to church soon, we'll be late."

That afternoon, Erica again battled with herself about telling her dad. Several times she opened her mouth, but the words died, unspoken.

Staring at her homework, she puzzled over why she felt so hesitant. Her dad had always been understanding. He wouldn't change now.

During dinner her father looked down at himself. "Do I have dirt on my face? Or did I forget to comb my hair?"

Erica looked at him intently. "No, you look fine. Why?"

"You keep looking at me as though I have a black bushy mustache or horns."

"Ah, Dad. She's in love," chimed in Alex. "This morning Pete and I were walking over on Cedar Street. We heard this loud yell, then a car pulled up next to the curb. It was Mike and Erica." His voice shuddered with disgust. "And he kissed her."

"Alex, I didn't see you."

"How could you? You were goggling at Mike."

"I was not. I'd just told him—well, I'd told him something special, and he was glad. You might mention that he kissed me on the forehead, not the lips."

Mr. Nelson grinned. "Sounds like Alex is going to have to do some sleuthing to discover what merited such a salute. Or are you going to share with us, too?"

A small voice inside Erica prompted, *Yes, tell them now. You promised.* Instead she said, "Soon. I'm not sure how to say it right now."

When she slipped into bed that evening, Erica held her new burgundy Bible. She turned the pages idly, reading a bit here and there as a phrase caught her eye. She stopped and read from Isaiah 26. "You will keep in perfect peace him whose mind is steadfast, because he trusts in you." And then a little further on, "The path of the righteous is level; O upright One, you make the way of the righteous smooth."

No wonder I don't have the peace I had yesterday, Erica thought. *I haven't been steadfast. I was weak and wishy-washy in not telling Dad. I'll do it tomorrow.*

Thinking about level paths and smooth ways, Erica fell asleep.

The next couple of days, it seemed that indeed her new Lord was making her paths straight. Her problems seemed to have receded, and Carolyn even smiled at her.

She hadn't told her dad yet, but she had told Leslie. "Being a Christian is wonderful," Erica said. "I wish you'd talk to Mrs. Havig and learn about it, too."

"I might," Leslie said, "after I see how it goes with you."

Wednesday morning, Erica found another note on her locker. Before opening it, she looked down at Leslie, who was kneeling to tie her shoe. "Mrs. Havig warned me that troubles might get bigger. I hope she's wrong."

Erica ripped open the envelope and silently read:

Don't think we've forgotten what your father has done—not the poster or his affair with the beautiful Valerie Donovan. We're working on proof now. Soon you'll pay.

Her hand trembled as she passed the note to Leslie.

When Leslie finished, she stuffed the piece of paper back into

Erica's hand. "I'd give my eyeteeth to know who's doing this. What are you going to do?"

"Give it to Dad. I promised I would." She shook her head. "If only we could catch someone at it. The only person in this hall when we came in was that redheaded kid. I don't even know his name, so why would he want to do something like this?"

"He could have been hired to," Leslie guessed, "but I'm still putting my money on Carolyn. She always seems to know what's going on in your life. I'll bet she makes some crack today."

Erica shrugged. "I don't know. I think she smiled at me yesterday."

"Sure, like a wolf smiles at a sheep."

"No, a friendly smile. Oh, I don't know. I could be wrong. We've got to run now, or we'll be late."

They separated and headed for their morning classes. On her way to Civics, Erica turned quickly when someone called her name. She banged her elbow against the fire extinguisher hanging on the wall. Pain shot through her arm and she gasped. Her head swam for a moment with pain, and she missed seeing whoever had called to her.

Later, in English class, she couldn't find her essay. She had finished it the night before, but it wasn't in her folder.

"This isn't like you, Erica," Miss Adams scolded. "I can usually count on you to be prepared."

Several of Erica's classmates snickered.

"I'm sorry, Miss Adams," Erica said, an unaccustomed chagrin flooding her. "I finished it last night. I just don't seem to have put it in my folder."

"Be sure it's here tomorrow," Miss Adams warned. "You know my rules."

Erica breathed a sigh of relief as she left school that day. *Not one more thing could possibly go wrong,* she thought.

But as she swung along the street on her way to *The Kerusso,* a car pulled up alongside. Carolyn leaned out the passenger window. "Careful, teacher's pet," she yelled. "You may lose Teach's approval. Get that homework caught up now." She cackled like a witch, and the driver honked repeatedly, then accelerated down the street.

Erica gritted her teeth. "Friendly smile, indeed. I'm going to get that girl if it's the last thing I do."

She ran the rest of the way to the office and burst in the front door. She barely acknowledged the greetings of the staff as she hurried back to her father's office with the note grasped in her hand.

She stopped abruptly. Alex was crouched close to the thin partition of their father's office, his ear to the wall.

14

"$\mathcal{A}$lex!" Erica exclaimed in a whisper. "What are you doing?"

He turned, his eyes snapping with excitement. He signaled frantically, one hand over his mouth, the other beckoning. Erica started toward him. The newspaper staff halted their work. The room became unnaturally silent.

Alex waved wildly at them, as though directing a strange orchestra. The staff, like obedient musicians, resumed their "playing." Computer monitors hummed, keyboards clicked, and talk resumed.

Erica slid to her knees beside Alex. "What is it?" she whispered.

He touched a finger to his lips, then wrote on his note pad, "Tyson's with Dad. Listen."

Erica nodded. "I'll go to my desk," she mouthed.

Alex shook his head, his hair bouncing. He pointed to the partition on the other side of their dad's cubbyhole office, jutting out from the rear wall of the big room.

Erica signaled with circled forefinger and thumb. She tiptoed to her desk, picked up a notebook and pencil, then moved around to the dark area stuffed with odds and ends of paraphernalia.

She settled on a box of paper in time to hear Tyson say, "You're a fool not to sell. I've been watching each edition get thinner with fewer advertisers." His harsh laugh rang out triumphantly. "I'll bet your circulation has dropped just as drastically."

Her father's voice was stony hard. "I assume there is a point to this conversation?"

"I'm trying to convince you you're in a losing proposition. But

I can bail you out." Tyson's oily voice made Erica shudder.

"Oh?" When Mr. Nelson used that tone, both Erica and Alex knew what it meant. Erica wished she could exchange glances with Alex.

"A couple months ago, I offered you $300,000 for *The Kerusso*." Tyson's repeated laugh grated on Erica's nerves. She wondered how her father could stand it. "I can't offer that anymore," he said, "but I will give you $75,000."

"*The Kerusso* is not for sale—at any price." Mr. Nelson's voice seemed remarkably calm. "Now, if that's all you came for, I have work to do," he said.

A chair scraped against the floor. Erica saw Tyson's silhouette, planting his hands on her father's desk and leaning threateningly forward. She jumped to her feet.

"That's not all, you fool," Tyson snarled. "I complained to you before about that son of yours. You tell him to keep his nose out of my business or I'll cut it off. Do you understand?"

"Alex is doing nothing illegal," Mr. Nelson replied, his voice cold with fury. "And if you insist on fighting, fight like a man—against another man, not against a mere boy." He stood. "This conversation is over. The door is behind you."

"You'll be sorry for this," Tyson threatened.

"Go!" Mr. Nelson commanded. "Now!"

Alex scrambled around the corner as the door flung open, banging against the partition. He grinned as Tyson, gray hair and beard bristling, strode through the office and slammed the front door behind him.

Erica and Alex hurried into their father's office. "Atta boy, Dad," encouraged Alex. "You told him."

Erica's eyes met her father's. "It'll be all right, Dad. He'll cool down. After all, he can't force you to sell."

"You heard?"

"Yes," said Erica. "We listened outside."

"Maybe I should sell," Mr. Nelson said, leaning back in his chair and closing his eyes. He blinked them open again. "He is right, you know. Circulation is down along with advertising. I'm just pouring your mother's money into a losing business. It can't go on."

"Don't give up yet, Dad." Alex looked anxiously at his father. "I think I can help you turn things around in less than a month."

Mr. Nelson grinned. Alex relaxed.

"I should know you'd never give in, son. In any case, I'd never sell to him. I'd close down first."

"Dad, just who is Tyson?" Erica asked. "What does he do?"

"He's a crook," Alex replied before his dad could answer.

Mr. Nelson shook his head. "That's a serious accusation, son. I just told Mr. Tyson you aren't doing anything illegal, so don't start now. I don't want a slander suit."

"It isn't slander if it's true. Within a month, I'll have all the proof I need."

Mr. Nelson's lips twitched. "Fine, Alex. But keep your accusations within the family until you have proof in your hand." His voice grew serious. "A suit for slander or defamation of character would be the last straw."

"Oh, Dad. I'm smarter than that," Alex protested.

"I still don't know who Tyson is," Erica said. "What does he do—other than being a crook?"

Mr. Nelson picked up a business card from his desk. "He's a land developer. I heard he's working on a couple projects, one on Orcas Island and another in the Everett area."

"That's a risky business right now, isn't it?" Erica asked.

"Yes, with money so tight, only a man with money behind him can venture a land deal of this magnitude. I assume Tyson has that money."

"I'll check," said Alex, jotting in his notebook.

Mr. Nelson shook his head. "Careful, son. Don't get into any more trouble. His money is none of our business. But, getting out *The Kerusso* is. Let's get to work."

———

After dinner that evening, Erica and her dad sat in the den reading, listening to music, and talking. Mr. Nelson stretched. "It's been quite a day. Not the best of days, but then, not the worst of days either."

Erica jumped up. "That reminds me." She hurried out and came back holding the note she had received that morning. "I almost forgot. This is what started off my less-than-perfect day."

Mr. Nelson took the note and read it. "You didn't see anyone hanging around?"

"No. Well, the redheaded kid was there. But I discovered he's a sophomore whose locker is just down from ours. I don't even know his name. I can't believe he's involved. He has no reason."

"Neither does anyone else we know. I'll file it with the others." He looked up at her. "You said the note was the beginning of a bad day. Anything else?"

"Just a lot of little things," Erica said. "I banged my elbow hard enough to make me dizzy. I forgot my English paper, and Miss Adams chewed me out in front of the class. Later, Carolyn called me 'teacher's pet.' Then I got to work and Tyson's threats. None of it is very big, but all together it made the whole day go wrong."

"I've had those days." Her father smiled. "Tomorrow is bound to be better. Things have a way of working out when you stand firm."

Standing firm, she thought. *That's the same as being steadfast.* Erica closed her book over her finger and looked at her dad. Her heart pounded, and a flush tinged her cheeks. She drew a deep breath. Day after tomorrow he'd be on his way to Boston. She just had to tell him before then.

"Something's bothering you, Erica," her father said. "I've noticed it since Saturday. Ready to tell me?"

Be steadfast. That's me, Erica thought. She looked her dad squarely in the eyes. "Yes, Dad. I don't know why I've been afraid to tell you," her voice lowered, "but I want you to know."

"Something wrong, Erica?"

"Oh no, Dad. This is good." Erica moved over to perch on the arm of his chair. She leaned her head on his shoulder for a moment, then straightened so she could see his face.

"Saturday, Mrs. Havig talked to me about being a Christian."

She paused, waiting for a reaction. Her father's face remained unchanged.

"Yes?" he prompted.

"I—I became a Christian, Dad. I invited Jesus to come into my life to be my Savior and Lord."

"Oh, my dear, that takes me back a long way." He slipped his arm around her. Erica thought she saw a tear glisten in his eye. Her own throat tightened.

"I did that when I was a young man," he continued, "not too long before I met your mother. I remember I bought a Bible—started reading it."

"I did that, too!" Erica exclaimed. "What happened, Dad? Why didn't you continue?"

"Well, the excitement of courtship and getting married, then jobs and school pressures for both of us, too little time for everything we needed and wanted to do." He sighed. "After that, careers and children."

"I'm sure it's not too late to begin again, Dad. Maybe we could learn together."

"Maybe, Erica. We'll see."

Erica hugged her father and kissed his forehead. "Thanks, Dad. I was hoping you'd understand." She started to leave the room but looked back from the doorway. "I'll be praying for you." The words felt good on her lips, and she smiled.

Friday afternoon, Erica stood at her locker, selecting the books she needed for homework over the weekend. Someone tapped her shoulder. She whirled to see Brian.

"Hi. Can I take my favorite girl out for a Coke?"

"Oh, Brian. I can't. I'm in a rush. I need to get home so I can take Dad to the airport, remember? He's going to Boston this weekend."

"Hand me your books and let's go. I'll drive you home and then out to the airport. Your dad won't mind."

"I guess you're right," Erica said, piling his arms with books. "In fact, he'll probably be delighted."

They had gone only a few steps when Leslie dashed up. "Leaving without me?" she called.

"I have to get Dad to the airport. Brian's giving me a lift. I'll talk to you tomorrow."

Brian raised his hand in salute, and Erica looked back to wave. The bleak look in Leslie's blue eyes distressed Erica. *It's Brian,* she thought. *Leslie is hurt because Brian came for me.*

At the airport, Erica clung to her father. Unlike her mother, Mr. Nelson didn't leave a list of dos and don'ts. He just hugged her tightly and said, "You'll do fine, Erica. I have every confidence in you."

"Hurry back, Dad," Erica said, her voice muffled in her father's shoulder. "I'm going to miss you terribly."

"I'll be here Sunday at eight. I'll meet you at the baggage claim."

"I'll be waiting." Erica wiped the tears from her lashes. "Have a good time, Dad."

"I will." He gave her one last squeeze and hurried through the jetway to the plane.

"How about that Coke on the way home?" Brian suggested.

"Okay," Erica said, "but I don't think any amount of Cokes could fill this empty feeling I have."

Brian reached over and took her hand. "It's only two days. You can handle that. In fact, ordinarily you'd be delighted to have this weekend to prove yourself."

Erica looked at him in surprise. He was right. Why was she feeling so down? Before she could think it through, they pulled into a fast-food restaurant, and Brian ordered two Cokes.

After they had talked for a moment, Brian said, "Karlotolo is the middle of next month. Do we have a date again this year?"

Erica swirled the ice in her cup with the straw. Finally she looked up. "I don't know, Brian. I'm not sure what to say."

"Yes would be a nice answer," Brian replied, his eyes refusing to meet hers.

Erica's heart twisted inside her. She hated to hurt Brian. He had been her best friend for so long. But now there was Mike—and

Leslie. Would life continue to grow more complicated?

She reached for Brian's hand. His quick answering squeeze intensified her inward pain.

"Does that mean yes?" he asked.

Indecision silenced Erica. She didn't want to miss Karlotolo—the most popular event of the Karston Founder's Festival. It was always an excellent local talent show with acts from operatic singers to guitarists to comics.

It was a dress-up affair after a day of parade, horse show, and air show. What if Mike didn't ask? Brian was a sure date. He was always fun to be with and attentive.

"Erica?" Brian prompted. "Is it Mike?"

Their eyes met. Erica read hurt on Brian's face and knew her own must reflect it. "Partly," she answered honestly. "I like him a lot. But it's something else, too. Something I'm not sure I have the right to tell you."

"Has our relationship changed so much that you can't confide in me anymore?"

"Oh no, it isn't that. There's just another person involved, and I'm not sure I should reveal someone else's feelings."

Brian looked puzzled.

Erica sighed. "Brian, I'm sorry. I may be doing the wrong thing, but I think I should say no."

"I don't get it, Erica, but I can see you're really struggling. I won't push anymore. I'm sorry you won't go with me. Maybe I'll skip it this year."

"You could ask someone else."

"Who? You're the only girl I'd enjoy being with."

"Yeah?" Erica said dryly. "If you think awhile, I'm sure you'll be able to think of someone else." She stood up. "I'd better get home, Brian. Alex will be chomping at the bit for dinner."

After dinner, Erica was cleaning the kitchen when the phone rang. As she picked up the receiver, Alex had already answered on the extension.

"Alex Nelson here," he said.

A man's voice she didn't recognize said, "Nelson. You're the kid who's been poking his nose into business that isn't his own, who thinks it's smart to go asking all kinds of questions around town."

Erica's hand crept up to her throat. Threat layered the man's voice like thick peanut butter.

Alex didn't seem to notice. "I've been doing some research," he replied jauntily. "Would you like a copy of my paper when I'm finished?"

"What I'd like is for you to butt out," growled the man. "Choose something else for your research and leave us alone."

"But I'm so far into this that I couldn't possibly stop now. It's getting most interesting."

Oh, Alex, Erica groaned silently, *don't antagonize him.*

"I'm telling you, kid. Knock it off or you'll be sorry." His voice grated with anger. "We know how to put an end to your activities if you don't."

"What? Erase my tape?" Alex goaded. "Wipe out my memory?"

"I've told you. Keep out or we'll keep you out." The man slammed down the phone.

Erica heard the gentler click of Alex's hanging up. *What should I do?* she wondered. *What would Dad do if he were home?* "Mom," she whispered, "it isn't fair of you to take him so far away—not now."

15

$\mathcal{E}$rica folded the dishcloth neatly and hung it over the sink. She wiped her hands and breathed, "Lord, show me what to do. Don't let me be bossy and make Alex angry."

Alex burst into the kitchen. "Erica! Did you hear? Isn't it great?"

"Great? I thought it was awful. Who was he?"

"I don't know, but I'll bet it's one of Tyson's thugs. That means I'm getting somewhere and they're worried."

"Don't push them, Alex. Remember what Dad said about getting into trouble."

"Ah, Erica, this is the time to push hard. Tomorrow Pete and I must put Plan C into effect. I'll call him."

"Alex," Erica stopped him. "Don't do anything foolish."

A disgusted look crept across Alex's face. "What do you think I am? Dumb?" He started down the stairs. "I need to do some checking and thinking. Relax. Everything's going to be okay."

Erica bit the inside of her lip until it stung. She didn't like the gleam in Alex's eyes and his determination to keep jabbing Tyson. Why did her mother have to be in Boston? And why did her dad have to pick this weekend to visit her?

The evening passed peacefully, and Erica began to relax. Alex pored over his notebook, making notes, fidgeting, planning—much as normal. She could almost see the tapes spinning in his mind.

The next morning, Alex handed Erica a page torn from his notebook. "Message for Pete. He's got chores this morning, but was supposed to meet me here at two. Change of plans," he said, "I have to get started now. Can you give this to him?"

"Sure."

"Promise? It's really important."

"I promised I'd spend some time with Mrs. Havig this afternoon," Erica replied. "If he doesn't come before I leave, I'll tape the note on the door. Okay?"

"Not the best, but it'll do."

"When will you be back?"

"Oh, late afternoon—in time for dinner at least."

Erica nodded. "See you then. Be careful."

Alex grimaced. "Of course," he said with intolerance. "I'm just after some information."

Erica waited for Pete as long as she could. Just as she taped Alex's note to the front door, the phone rang. She dashed inside.

"Erica, it's Les. Oh, Erica! Guess what?"

"Slow down. What is it?"

"The best thing in the whole world. Brian asked me to Karlotolo!" Leslie fairly squealed in her excitement. "I have to have a new dress. Will you help me find one this afternoon?"

"I can't, Les. I'm on my way out to Havigs'. I promised Ellen. You can find a dress without me."

"No. I'll wait. When will you be home?"

"Probably too late to shop. How about next week?"

"Okay." Disappointment flattened Leslie's voice. "Can't you get out of going to Havigs'?"

"I don't want to," Erica said. "I want to spend some time with Ellen. I've already learned so much about the Bible. I'm sorry, Les, but I can't do it today."

As she drove toward the Havig place, a tiny bit of remorse crept around Erica's heart. What if Mike didn't ask her to the Karlotolo? She'd hate to go alone, or not at all. The thought of shopping with Leslie for a special dress if she didn't need one herself tore at her.

It was a relief to step into the warm, loving atmosphere of Ellen's kitchen, where books were spread out on the table and fresh cookies and cupcakes cooled on the counter.

Ellen welcomed her with a quick hug. "A glass of milk and a cupcake?" she asked.

"Yes, thank you."

"How did it go this week?"

Erica frowned. "A lot of bad things happened." Her face lightened in surprise. "But the overall feeling is good. I don't understand."

"It's the peace I told you about," Ellen said. "Peace beyond our understanding keeps us from going under even when bad things happen. Would you like to tell me what happened?"

Erica told her about the latest note, the small disasters of Wednesday, and Tyson's threats. She ended with the worrisome phone call Alex had received the night before.

"I don't know what to do. I warned him not to hassle Tyson anymore, but I'm afraid my words went in one ear and out the other."

Erica's anger rose. "Oh, I wish I didn't have all this responsibility. I feel so alone." Her eyes burned with unexpected tears. "I wish Mom and Dad were here, not thousands of miles away. Why can't my mom be like you?"

"Hush, Erica," Ellen replied gently. "No," she corrected herself. "That isn't what I mean. Let's talk about it."

Erica looked up expectantly.

"First, you're not alone. You have Jesus and His Holy Spirit to supply everything you need."

Ellen poured more milk into their glasses. "That's part of what I wanted to share with you during our Saturday afternoons. But more important, I don't think you really know what you're saying."

Erica studied Ellen thoughtfully. "I'm saying I would like my mother to be like you—motherly, caring, more concerned about her family than anything else."

"Yes," replied Ellen, her voice gentle. "But you're also saying that God made a mistake in giving you the mother He did."

"I guess I am saying that," Erica said.

"Hard as it may seem, God knew which mother would bring you to the place where He wants you to be."

"I never thought of it that way," Erica replied. "Did God really choose Mom for me for a special reason?"

"Of course. Nothing happens to us by mere chance. It's all covered by God's overall plan for our lives."

"How can I change my attitude?"

"We'll start by making it a matter of prayer. That reminds me," she interrupted herself, "how was your quiet time this week?"

"Good, I think," Erica replied, "but I may have done it wrong."

Ellen laughed. "As long as you're reading God's Word and spending time in prayer and praise, you can't be wrong."

Erica opened her journal notebook and Bible, relating some of the things she had learned that week from reading the first three chapters of John.

"That's wonderful, Erica," Ellen encouraged. "I can see that God's Spirit is already teaching you many things." She moved closer to be able to see Erica's open Bible. "Did you happen to notice verse twenty-seven in the third chapter?"

"Let me see. . . ." Erica found the place and began reading aloud. " 'A man can receive only what is given him from heaven—' " Erica looked up. "Oh," she said, "that proves what you said a few minutes ago. God did give Mom to me. That's the only way I could have gotten her."

"Right," said Ellen. "It could also include all the troubles you and your family are experiencing right now. God allows these things to happen for a purpose."

Erica made some notes in her journal.

"Why don't we pray about it together?" Ellen offered.

"You mean both of us, out loud?" Erica asked.

Ellen laughed. "It's not as scary as it sounds," she assured her. "We pray to God just like you and I would talk together. We tell Him our troubles, desires, hopes, and joys."

Erica was a little frightened at first, but as they prayed together, she forgot about what Ellen might think and frankly talked to the Lord about her concerns.

All too soon it was time to go. She drove home, put the car in the garage, and walked into the house.

"Alex, are you here?" she called.

The house was silent. She ran down to her room, stopping to

knock at Alex's door on the way. No answer. She put her Bible and notebook in her room, then went up to the kitchen.

She had just taken meat from the refrigerator to make hamburgers when the phone rang.

A man's deep voice asked, "Is this Erica Nelson?"

"Yes," she replied.

"This is Officer Shipman—Karston Police."

Erica's heart beat wildly. "Alex," she whispered. "Has he been hurt?"

"Physically, he's fine," the officer assured her. "We're holding him for burglary."

"Alex? Oh no! He wouldn't."

"He did. We picked him up in the office of Tyson and Associates. I understand your parents are in Boston."

Erica had trouble breathing. "Yes. Mom works there. Dad will be back tomorrow night. What can I do?"

"Normally, we don't release kids to minors, but Chief Murphy would like you to come down and talk to us. Alex claims he has a good reason for having entered Tyson's office, but he won't tell. All he'll say is he promised his father. Maybe he'll talk to you."

"I'll be there as soon as I can," Erica promised.

Her heartbeat slowed dramatically. She seemed to be moving in slow motion. What should she do? Automatically, she put the meat away. She ran down for her coat, purse, and car keys, then paused by the phone. She'd call Mike.

She waited impatiently. The phone rang and rang. Just as she was about to give up, Mike's brother Geoff answered.

"Hi, Geoff. This is Erica. Is Mike there?"

"Yeah, hold on."

Something inside Erica cried, *Hurry, hurry!* Her fingers dangled the car keys, grabbed them, dangled them, and grabbed them again.

"Erica. How are you?" Mike's voice conveyed genuine concern.

"I have to cancel our date tonight," Erica apologized.

"What's up?"

Erica wet her lips. "I just got a call from the police station. They're holding Alex on a burglary charge. I'm going to try to get him out. The officer sounded like he might release him to me, but I'm not sure, since I'm a minor. I have to talk to the Chief of Police, and it may take some time."

"That dumb kid. I told him not to try it."

"You knew he was going to do something?"

"I thought I'd talked him out of it. I'll—"

"Listen, I'd better go," Erica interrupted.

"Want me to go with you?"

"No. I'd better do it myself. Thanks."

"Erica, I'll be praying. We all will."

As Erica headed for the police station, she prayed. "Father, help me. I don't know about police stations and procedures. The officer sounded so grim, as if Alex is in terrible trouble. Would you straighten things out?"

When she reached City Hall, she found a parking space and walked toward the white-fronted building. In all the years she had lived in Karston, she had never been inside.

Taking a deep breath, Erica pulled open the door and stepped into a narrow hall with pass-through windows on either side. She searched for an identifying sign. She had just glimpsed "POLICE" on a white cardboard when a short, round woman stepped into the hall.

"May I help you?" she asked with a friendly smile.

"I'm looking for the police department."

The woman pointed toward the back of the hall where Erica had seen the sign.

Erica nodded. A few people sat in the offices on either side. Her eyes swept their faces as she passed. No one she knew.

Broad lines in three shades of blue followed the stairwell down to a lower floor. On the landing midway, the lines spelled out the word POLICE again. Even the bright colors and modern graphics didn't hide the antique dinginess.

The stairway ended in a small room, empty except for a couple of chairs and a small desk. Off to the right there was another small room. Inside, two uniformed officers sat busily writing.

Are they writing about Alex? she wondered. *Where is he?*

One of the men looked up and smiled. "I'm Officer Shipman. May I help you?"

"I'm Erica Nelson. You called about my brother, Alex."

"Oh yes." He stood and motioned for her to follow him.

She stepped into the room. Through another open doorway she saw Alex hunched over on a chair by a desk.

He looked up and tried to smile, but it was a far cry from his normal happy-go-lucky grin.

Erica tried to control her anger as she walked over to him. "Why, Alex? Why? You had to know it was wrong. And you promised Dad."

Alex looked miserable.

Officer Shipman intervened. "Chief Murphy, this is Alex's sister, Erica Nelson."

Erica's eyes flicked to the corner behind the desk. Chief Murphy stood and reached to shake her hand. He wasn't as tall as Officer Shipman, but he gave the impression of power. He rocked back on his heels, his hands resting on the wide, black belt that carried his gun.

"Alex, here"—the chief's shoulder twitched in Alex's direction—"has been fairly cooperative. He didn't resist arrest, and he wasn't carrying a weapon."

Indignation colored Erica's voice. "Of course he wasn't! Why should he?"

"You'd be surprised how many kid burglars carry knives, or chains, or whatever. Anyway, Alex didn't have any. He tells me he wanted information—not to steal. But taking information is stealing." The chief's big fingers tapped his belt buckle. "That's immaterial, of course. The charge is breaking and entering, regardless of why he did it."

Erica swallowed hard. "Can I take him home?"

"Sorry. We need more facts. He refuses to tell us why—what information he was after. He insists he can't break a promise to his father, even to keep from going to juvenile detention."

Alex broke in. "Dad told me not to say anything outside the family. Remember, Erica? He didn't want a slander suit along with everything else."

Chief Murphy looked at Erica.

She took a deep breath. "Can we express an opinion to you without it being slander?"

The police chief relaxed. His brown eyes became friendly. "At the risk of slander myself, I don't think anything you could say against Tyson could be called slander."

Erica turned to Alex. "I don't think Dad would hold you to your promise, Alex. Please tell him."

"The chief didn't say he wouldn't charge us with slander," Alex pointed out.

"Not in so many words, did I?" agreed Chief Murphy. "Okay, this will be an off-the-record conversation. You're safe."

Alex regained most of his usual jauntiness. "Tyson is a crook. I know he is. I just don't have any proof yet. Our dad runs *The Kerusso*."

"I know."

"Well, most of the advertisers have quit advertising, and each week more and more people cancel subscriptions, though that's not as bad as the advertisers."

"I had noticed the paper looked different," Officer Shipman said, "but I hadn't paid any attention to why. What does that have to do with Tyson?"

"Tyson is threatening anyone who advertises in *The Kerusso*. I have only one businessman, perhaps two, who might testify to that. The others are too scared. And the two who are willing won't testify unless we can guarantee that Tyson won't carry out his threats."

"Threats?"

"Tyson threatened to do to their businesses what he's done to our paper—make it go bankrupt."

"But your dad is still publishing."

"Yeah, but only because Mom makes so much money that we can afford to take a loss on the paper." Alex's eyes shone with pride. "Otherwise, we'd be broke and Dad would have to sell to Tyson."

"All this is very interesting," said Chief Murphy. "Did you find what you were looking for?"

"I didn't have much time," mumbled Alex, looking at his shoes. "The silent alarm brought the police so fast I didn't have a chance."

The chief's brown eyes twinkled. "I guess it doesn't matter. Thank you, son, for being so helpful." He turned to Erica. "When will your father be back?"

"Tomorrow evening on the eight o'clock flight."

"Is there anywhere we can reach him now?"

Erica checked her watch. Five-thirty. "It's eight-thirty in Boston. They'll be at the dinner. I don't know where it's being held or how long it will last. You could reach him at Mom's apartment later tonight or tomorrow."

Erica's eyes met the chief's. He smiled. "You appear to be a responsible young lady. I'll let Alex go home with you. But I want to see both Alex and your father on Monday. Have your father call to arrange a time."

"Thank you, sir," Erica said in a businesslike tone. "I promise to keep him with me until Dad gets home."

Alex jumped out of his chair and walked to the door. Erica followed. She turned back to thank Chief Murphy again and caught a speculative look before he wiped his face of expression and waved. She nodded and hurried after Alex.

In the car, Alex breathed a fervent, "Thanks, sis." Then they were both silent.

Erica kept trying to decide what she should say, how much she should say, or whether she should say anything at all. The two reached home without saying much to each other. They were hardly inside the door when the doorbell rang.

When Erica answered it, Brian smiled at her. "Mike asked me to keep a lookout for you. When I saw you drive in, I gave him a call, then came over. He's picking up Leslie and coming, too."

Erica gave him a grateful smile. "Alex and I haven't had dinner. How about you?"

"Hollow as a rain barrel. Should we send out for pizza?"

"No. We have hot dogs in the fridge. Why don't you start a fire downstairs? We'll make a picnic of it."

"Super." Brian disappeared downstairs with Alex. Erica heard them arranging wood in the fireplace. She filled a tray with wieners, buns, pickles, and olives, tossed a bag of potato chips on top, and took a six-pack of Pepsi from the refrigerator.

Just then Mike and Leslie arrived. Leslie threw her arms around Erica and all in one breath cried, "Are you okay? How could Alex do such a thing?"

Mike squeezed Erica's shoulder. "It must have gone okay. I hear Alex."

"They let me bring him home," she said. "But it's not over. He's in serious trouble. Burglary is a felony. The only thing in his favor was his cooperation with the police."

Mike's arm slipped around Erica. He drew her close. "We'll be praying," he said in her ear. "It'll come out for the best."

They walked into the kitchen, and Leslie spied the tray of food. "Oh, good. I missed dinner to come over. When do we eat?"

"Soon," said Erica. "Brian and Alex are building a fire." She picked up the tray and then set it down. "Reaction seems to be setting in. I'm shaking. Mike, would you?"

"Sure. Are you okay?"

"I will be. Let's go downstairs. Les, you take that big bowl for popcorn. I can manage the Pepsi."

Brian and Alex's fire crackled a welcome. Brian grinned at the newcomers. "Ah, food. We'll have to wait for this to burn down some."

"We can get things ready," Erica said. "Oh, Alex, I forgot paper plates and the knives."

"I'll get them." Alex left.

Brian looked at Erica. "Alex didn't say a word. Is he okay?"

"I don't know," said Erica. "It could be bad." She stopped as she heard his steps clattering down the stairs.

Conversation awkwardly avoided any mention of Alex's predicament, but after they'd eaten, Mike put his hand on Alex's shoulder. "Want to talk about it?"

"Are you going to say 'I told you so'?"

"Would it help?"

"No."

"Then I'll let it pass. Did you get your information?"

Alex nodded, eyes sparkling. "Bozeman. The town is Bozeman. I'd just found it when the police came. If only they'd been a couple minutes longer."

"How did you get in?" asked Leslie. "Break a window?"

"Of course not," Alex replied in disgust. "I used my plastic student ID card. I've seen people open doors with credit cards on TV lots of times. I practiced at home until I could do it. It's easy."

"Not a skill the police would be delighted to have every seventh-grader know," remarked Brian. "What did they say? The police, I mean."

"The ones who picked me up didn't say much. Just searched me and pushed me down the stairs and into their car. Nothing rough. Just heavy handed, like Dad when I'm out of line."

Alex put his hands over his ears. "But that Officer Shipman. He really gave me a tongue lashing. He must get a lot of practice. He's better than Dad. My ears still hurt."

"They should," said Erica.

Mike frowned at her and shook his head. "What else?"

"They called Erica."

Erica toyed with her necklace. "And I don't know what to do now," she said. "I suppose I should call Dad."

"What for? You'll just ruin his weekend," Alex complained.

"Me ruin his weekend? I think you're the one who's done that."

"Wait, Erica," Mike said. "What could your dad do, catch an earlier flight home? He'll be here in—" he checked his watch—"less than twenty-four hours. I'd hold off."

"I agree," Leslie said. "Let him enjoy Boston."

Erica looked at Brian. He nodded agreement.

Erica sighed. "I guess you're right. He'll find out soon enough. If Mom weren't so selfish, none of this would have happened."

"Come off it, Erica. Mom has nothing to do with it. Here or in Boston. It's all my fault!" Alex jumped up and left the room, slamming the door behind him.

"He's right, Erica," said Brian. "I think it's time you quit blaming your mother for everything that goes wrong. Be glad for what you have—friends and your father's trust."

Erica stared at him in disbelief. "I thought you were my friend."

"He is!" snapped Leslie. "I agree with him. It's all in your head."

Erica turned numbly to Mike. Would he agree, too?

Mike reached out and took her hand. "We're not in your situation, Erica. So we can't understand totally, but maybe you should reconsider your feelings about your mother. God gave her to you. He did it for a special purpose."

"Your mother told me the same thing," she said, clinging to his hand. "I've started to pray about it, but I guess I haven't changed much yet."

Mike squeezed her hand. "It'll come. Now, how about calling Alex back and playing some games?"

16

$\mathcal{E}$rica woke Alex early the next morning.

"I don't want to go to church," he protested. "I have things to think about."

"Sorry, brother. I promised Chief Murphy you wouldn't get into trouble. The only way I can keep my promise is to keep you in sight every minute. You're going."

"Oh, all right," Alex grumbled. "But I wouldn't do anything. You'd think I'd committed a crime or something."

"You did! A serious one. Now, get ready. Mike will be here soon."

When Mike arrived, Alex clambered into the backseat while Erica slid into the front. At the corner, they turned the opposite way from the church.

"I'm picking up Carolyn White," Mike explained. "She called this morning for a ride."

"Carolyn?" Erica looked startled.

"Isn't she the one who's writing those notes?" asked Alex.

"Hush, Alex. We don't know for sure," said Erica. "It could be the red-haired boy or someone we don't know."

They pulled up in front of Carolyn's house. Ranks of crocuses bloomed along the walk up to the front door. A forsythia waved yellow arms at the corner of the house. The two-car garage gaped emptily. A curtain twitched aside. They waited. Carolyn didn't come.

Mike opened his door. "I'll see what's keeping her."

He knocked and the door flew open. Carolyn came out, her black hair smooth and shining, her red dress a dream of perfection.

Erica's hands clenched as Carolyn clung to Mike's arm and he escorted her to the car. He opened the rear door for her. For the first time, Carolyn's face betrayed anger. She slid into the backseat. "Oh, Erica, the little half-orphan. Is this your brother?"

"Good morning, Carolyn," said Erica, fighting an angry retort. "Yes, this is Alex. Alex, Carolyn White. She's in my class at school."

Alex's eyes revealed that the facade hadn't fooled him. In one quick glance, he had obviously judged her and found her wanting.

Erica breathed a sigh of relief when Alex turned to the window. He was quite capable of a scathing remark that would start a verbal battle.

At church, Carolyn managed to manipulate things so that Erica entered the pew first, followed by Alex, herself, and then Mike. Erica bowed her head and whispered, "Lord, I can't pretend I don't care. Just don't let me get mad at her, please."

After the service, Alex fidgeted beside Erica as she talked to Becky, Mike's great pinch-hit piano player.

Within minutes, Carolyn came up. "Mike is ready to go," she said. "Can you tear yourself away?"

Erica swung around. "Come on, Alex." She stared Carolyn straight in the eye, then relaxed. "Sure. We're ready. Are you?"

She felt Becky's hand on her shoulder. Turning to say goodbye, Erica caught Becky's approving wink. She walked to the door—Carolyn on one side, Alex on the other. Erica kept her hand on Alex's arm, silently warning him not to start a fight.

When they got to the car, Mike wasn't there. "Oh," Carolyn purred, "he must have gone to look for me. Well, I'll wait in the front seat. You two can share the back." She opened the door and gracefully slipped in.

"Wait with her?" muttered Alex. "Nothing doing. I'll go find Mike."

Erica started to follow Alex, changed her mind, and slid into the backseat.

"Where did Alex go?" snapped Carolyn. "I can't wait here forever."

"Just to find Mike. He'll get here when Mike does."

"It does give us a chance to talk privately," Carolyn said, her voice changing from waspish to honey. "There's something I think you should know, and I never see you alone." She twisted around in the seat to face Erica.

"Yes?" Erica asked, not wanting to hear.

"It's about your dating Mike."

Anger flushed Erica's cheeks. "Yes?" she repeated.

"You'd make it a whole lot easier for him if you'd cool it. He isn't supposed to be taking you out."

"What do you mean?"

"I didn't think you knew," Carolyn said, satisfaction purring in her voice. "The whole church is praying about it, especially the young people's group. I hear his folks are frantic."

Pain twisted in Erica's heart. She clenched her hands. "I don't know what you're talking about."

"I knew you wouldn't. Mike is rebelling against both his parents and God because he refuses to stop seeing you. I guess . . ." Carolyn's voice trailed off.

Erica held herself against the pain as Mike and Alex bounded across the parking lot and got into the car. Mike's eyes met Erica's in the rear-view mirror. She forced a smile.

Carolyn smirked with satisfaction. "We've been talking, and we decided it would be better if you dropped off the orphans first, then take me home. It's more on your way. We're so grateful for your giving us rides, we want to make things easiest for you."

With another questioning glance at Erica through the mirror, Mike turned the key and started the car.

Erica closed her eyes for a moment as a sick feeling swept through her.

If I'm causing him to sin, she thought, *I've got to stop seeing him.* Her heart twisted again. *Does that mean I can't spend my Saturdays with Ellen either?*

After Mike dropped them off, Alex said, "Boy, she's really a witch, isn't she? Why'd you keep me from getting back at her?"

"I don't know, Alex. Even when she was hurting me—us—

something inside stopped me. By the way, I really need to stop complaining about Mom. I'm sorry for what I said last night about her," she apologized. "I've gotten into a rut on this. I'm trying to change."

"Good," said Alex. "Mom's not so bad. She's just Mom, like you're Erica. You are who you are."

"That's rather profound," Erica teased to cover the lump in her throat. She tousled his hair. "How did you get so much wiser than I am?"

Alex pulled away. "No need to get mushy," he said, heading down to his room.

Erica took her Bible to her room and then started for the kitchen when the phone rang.

Alex answered it.

"Oh, that's great," she heard him say. "No, I don't need to ask her. She'll agree. See you."

"Alex," Erica called. "You know you can't go anywhere until Dad gets home."

"You're going, too," Alex explained, coming into the kitchen. "That was Mrs. Havig. She wants us to come for dinner. Mike's coming to pick us up."

"Oh," Erica said, glowing.

Maybe Carolyn had tricked her again, because Erica and Alex enjoyed a lovely meal at the Havigs' without any indication of trouble.

———

Mike took them home on his way to the youth meeting. Alex disappeared inside the house immediately, but Erica lingered for a moment.

Mike walked her to the door. "I'm sorry you have to miss tonight. Next week?" he asked.

"Yes," she said. "Now you'd better scoot or you'll be late. Besides, it's time for us to pick up Dad. I'm really looking forward to having him home, but I dread telling him about Alex."

Mike bent swiftly and kissed her. "I'll be praying." He jumped off the porch and ran toward his car. He waved as he drove off.

Erica watched his car disappear down the street and found doubts creeping back in. *Is there anything to what Carolyn said?* she wondered. Should she stop seeing him?

————

On the way to the airport, Erica suggested, "Let's not say anything about the burglary until we get home. We'll keep Dad talking about Mom and Boston."

Alex's face brightened. "Thanks, Erica. I've been dreading this more and more as the afternoon passed," he confessed. "It would be easier to tell him at home than while driving down the freeway."

Erica parked the car in one of the metered spots at the end of the terminal, and they walked to the luggage area.

"Do you think he'll just look at me and know?" Alex verbalized his worry.

Erica smiled in sympathy. "No. Your guilt isn't written all over your face."

They looked up. Mr. Nelson strode across from the escalator and put an arm around each of them. He hugged them tightly. "I'm delivering that hug for your mother," he said huskily. "She told me to tell you she misses you terribly."

The familiar, *Oh, yeah?* rose to Erica's lips, but she squelched it and smiled at her dad.

As soon as his luggage arrived, they left the terminal.

"Tell us about your weekend, Dad," Alex said. "What did you and Mom do?"

Mr. Nelson told them all about the sights they'd visited and the people he'd met. Whenever he lapsed, one or the other would ask a new question, and he would continue talking.

At one point he stretched and said, "Well, enough about me. How was your weekend?"

Alex caught Erica's eye in consternation. Erica took one hand from the wheel and touched her father's. "We can tell you about us later. We're hungry for news of Mom."

Mr. Nelson looked doubtfully at Erica. "Do I sense a change in attitude?"

Erica nodded. "Yes, that's one of the things I want to talk to you about, but later. Tell us more."

The words and miles clicked away. At home, Alex started a fire in the rec room while Erica prepared a snack. Her dad carried the tray downstairs.

"It's sure good to get home," Mr. Nelson said, plopping down in an easy chair and stretching his feet toward the fire. "It would be perfect if your mother were here."

"Well, not quite perfect, Dad," said Erica. "We still have our share of troubles."

Her father looked up. "What happened while I was gone?"

Erica looked at Alex, then started, "Well—"

"No, Erica. It's my story," Alex said. He squared his shoulders and moved to stand in front of his dad. "I did a dumb thing, Dad, even after I promised you I wouldn't get into trouble. I was trying to get some information to solve the Tyson case, but it didn't work quite right."

Mr. Nelson's eyes narrowed. His fingers pulled at his earlobe. "You'd better tell me about it, son."

"You know I lost the name of that town in Montana where my trail on Tyson led. I had to get it again, and the only way was to go to Tyson's office and find it." Alex shifted to the other foot. "So, that's what I did."

"Yes?"

"Pete helped me. He called Tyson's three goons and told them he was Tyson. He ordered them to meet him at three o'clock in the old vacant warehouse north of town. Then Pete called Tyson and whispered, 'If you want ammunition that will make *The Kerusso* fold, meet me at the vacant warehouse, three o'clock.' He hung up before Tyson could ask any questions."

"All of this so you could get into his office when no one was there?" his father prodded.

"Yes, and it worked." A flash of light reflected in Alex's eyes. "I wish I could have seen that meeting!"

Mr. Nelson relaxed. "It sounds like you watch too much TV," he said, "but go on."

"When I got to the office, it was empty. I used my plastic student ID card to get in—the way they do on TV." He spread out his hands. "Just one problem. When I opened the door, it set off a silent alarm. I'd just found the town name in a file when the police burst in."

"Police?"

"Yes. They searched me, took me down to the station, and turned me over to Officer Shipman. Boy, did he yell at me." Alex covered his ear. "I think I still have blisters."

"I should add a few more—to a different part of your anatomy," Mr. Nelson said, shaking his head. "Alex, how could you?"

"The detectives on TV do it all the time. Nothing happens to them."

"But that's television, not real life," Dad protested.

"That's what I told him," Erica said.

"What's the outcome?"

"Chief Murphy agreed to release him to me after we talked." Erica took a deep breath. "Alex has been charged with burglary, and you have to call the police station tomorrow." She handed her father Chief Murphy's card.

He took it and looked at it as though he weren't seeing it. After a long silence, which made Alex squirm and Erica want to spring to his defense, Mr. Nelson looked at Alex.

"I guess you know that you have been inexcusably foolish. Worse, you've infringed on another's right of privacy."

"But, Dad. He's a crook!"

"That doesn't negate his rights."

"Don't I have a responsibility to help the authorities bring him to justice if I can?" Alex persisted.

"Yes, but within the law, Alex. *Within* the law, not using the same tactics the crooks use." Dad stood and put his hand on Alex's shoulder. "I think the police will take care of your punishment. But, from now on, you're not to go near Mr. Tyson. You're not to call him, pester him, even see him. If he comes near you, you move. Do you understand?"

"Yes, Dad."

"Do I have your word?"

"Yes. I won't bother Mr. Tyson anymore."

"One more thing, son."

"Yes?"

"When you need to accomplish something, there's always a right way and a wrong way. The wrong way is never justified. You must search and wait for the right way. Remember that."

"Yes, Dad." Alex nodded. "It'll be a while before I could forget. I won't do anything like this ever again."

Mr. Nelson grew even more serious and for several minutes looked from one of his children to the other. "This whole thing is getting completely out of hand. Let's close down the paper and move to Boston. Your mother doesn't have to come back here. Her job could be in Boston just as well."

"Oh, Dad, no!" cried Erica. "You can't. Not now."

Alex joined her protest. "You can't run away from Tyson. Give up and let the bad guy win? That's as bad as getting the information the wrong way." Alex hopped up and down in his excitement. "I've got the name of the town now, and something more. I found out that Mr. Tyson sometimes goes by the name of Tyler. Don't move us now, Dad. Please."

"I haven't made a decision yet. But if much more goes wrong, we're leaving!"

17

On Monday afternoon, in the midst of the bustle and turmoil of getting the paper ready for the presses, the outer door burst open and slammed shut.

Erica looked up. The man striding across the room had blazing red hair and furious red-brown eyes. Even his freckles danced angrily across his face. In his hand was a piece of poster board.

Erica stood up. "Senator Palmer?"

He brushed her aside and pushed his way into her father's cubbyhole office.

"Where's Alex?" Erica whispered to a keyboardist.

Shouts from her father's office drowned out her answer and brought Alex rushing from the pressroom.

"What's going on?" he demanded.

"Senator Palmer just barged in," Erica said. "He had one of those posters in his hand. What should we do?"

"Listen." Alex moved to the storage area and hunched over his note pad.

Erica followed.

Senator Palmer wasn't yelling anymore, but his loud, angry voice carried over the busy noises of the newspaper office.

"Why are you trying to ruin me? What's in it for you?" he demanded. "You're a low-down, dirty skunk. If I'd been in town lately, you'd never have gotten away with this so long."

Though Erica strained, she couldn't hear her father's quiet reply.

As though in response to that soft answer, Senator Palmer's voice again dropped in volume. "Then what about this?" he ground out. "Your name's on this one."

Again, a quiet reply from their father.

"You expect me to believe that?" Senator Palmer's voice rose. "If you'd blast me in your newspaper, why not an anonymous poster?"

Before Erica knew what he was doing, Alex dashed into their father's office. "Don't be so dumb!" he shouted. "If Dad were going to print that poster, he wouldn't have run such an editorial two days before."

"Enough, Alex," Mr. Nelson ordered. "Apologize."

Erica peered around the corner of the partition.

Alex mumbled, "I'm sorry," then looked up at Senator Palmer. "But you should know better. Even if he weren't my dad, I could figure out that someone had read the editorial and used it for their own ends. Who hates you that much?"

Erica saw surprise and then amusement cross Senator Palmer's face.

Mr. Nelson reached out and grabbed Alex's shoulder. "I said *enough*, son. We don't talk to people that way."

But Senator Palmer smiled broadly, his anger forgotten. He turned to Mr. Nelson. "I wish my son would champion me to that degree. I'm afraid I don't rank so high with Jerry."

His face grew grim. "I don't know who hates me," he replied to Alex's question. "I was so furious before. I really believed your dad did this, but now I can see your logic."

Erica stepped behind her brother. "A lot of people who have nothing to be angry about also believe we were responsible for the poster."

Mr. Nelson raised his hand. "I'd like to work this out with you, Senator Palmer. But if the paper, or what's left of it, is to come out on time, I've got to get busy. And so do these kids of mine."

"What's left of your paper—what do you mean?" asked Palmer.

"It seems your enemy is my enemy. Since that editorial and the poster episode, we've lost almost all our advertisers and a good number of our subscribers. In short, we're all but bankrupt."

Senator Palmer looked puzzled. "What's the connection? We

haven't had much to do with each other, except those ads I ran during my last campaign. I think we need to continue this discussion."

"I agree," said Mr. Nelson. "How about dinner tonight at our home?"

"Not tonight. I'm already committed." Senator Palmer reached into his pocket for an appointment calendar and flipped it open. "I'm free Thursday night."

"Fine," Mr. Nelson said. "Bring your wife." He stood to shake hands with the Senator. "I'm looking forward to talking with you."

Senator Palmer turned and shook hands with both Erica and Alex. "See you all on Thursday."

———

Later on that afternoon Mr. Nelson and Alex went to the police station to see Chief Murphy.

Alex told Erica about it later. "Mr. Boxer, the county prosecutor, sure had me scared," Alex said. "He started by talking about the worst possible punishment—going through court and being sentenced to the detention home. Then he worked his way down to the least."

"What did he decide?"

"Something called diversion. He said that since I'm a first offender and not likely to do it again, I just have to see a probation officer once a month for three months and do some kind of community service. I'm not sure what that will be yet." Alex shrugged. "At least we can keep it out of the paper. Dad certainly won't print it, and the city papers don't carry little stuff like this."

Erica breathed a sigh of relief. "That was too close, Alex. But I'm glad things seem to be working out," she said. "Now if we could just get back our advertisers, everything would be fine, and Dad would forget about going to Boston."

———

Thursday afternoon, during a meeting in her father's office, the phone rang. Erica answered. She handed the receiver to her dad.

"It's John Blake, the City Attorney."

"Richard Nelson here," her father said.

The staff continued their discussion in low voices as Mr. Nelson listened to the City Attorney. Erica watched her father's face grow grim. After what seemed like a very long time, he said, "I understand. I'll be in your office within half an hour."

He hung up. Turning to the staff he said, "When the garbage crew picked up our trash today, one of the men found the printing plate of the poster that libeled Palmer."

A shock of disbelief passed through the room.

"A plant," grunted Alex. "Whoever made the posters feels now is a good time to wipe us out. He could have planted the evidence weeks ago. He waited until now. I wonder why?"

Mr. Nelson jumped to his feet. "Someone has gone too far. I'm getting to the bottom of this." He grabbed his coat from the rack in the corner and strode to the door. "I'll see you in the morning."

When Erica got home, she dialed the Havigs' number.

Mike answered. "Hi, Erica."

"Is your mom there? I want her to pray about something."

"What's up?"

"Someone put the printing plate used to make the Palmer poster in the dumpster we use at *The Kerusso* and made sure it would be found. Dad is being accused. He's still at the City Attorney's office."

"What can I do?"

"Ask your mother to pray, would you?"

"Of course." Mike answered. "We'll all pray—a family project. Anything else we can do?"

"Not now. We'll know more about it when Dad gets home."

"This might not be the time to ask," Mike said, "but I was planning to call you later to see if you'd like to go to a Christian concert with me tomorrow night. I was just given some tickets."

"I'd love to," Erica said, forgetting her concern about dating him again. "But can I let you know for sure after we find out what's going to happen?"

"Sure. Remember, we'll be praying."

"Thanks, Mike."

Erica hung up and switched on the TV news. She plopped down on a chair and listened with little interest as a state legislator talked about rising taxes and hope for new cuts.

Then she heard, "This afternoon at a meeting of the Karston City Council, the regular agenda was interrupted by Mr. Bert Tyson. Following an anonymous tip, our cameras were there."

The cameras focused on a man of medium height, with gray hair and a beard which couldn't hide his thin, cruel lips. They curled upward in what passed for a smile, but no smile touched his penetrating eyes.

"I'm afraid it's bad news this afternoon, friends and fellow citizens of Karston," Tyson began. "I'm speaking on behalf of our esteemed Senator Ralph Palmer, who is striving for our good in the state legislature. Several weeks ago a vicious campaign to smear his name was instituted and came to a head with ugly, libelous posters asking for his recall."

The camera pulled in for a close-up of Tyson's face as he continued. "Today, we have evidence that points directly to the source of the attack—one thought to be an upstanding member of our community—Mr. Richard Nelson, owner, publisher, and editor of *The Karston Kerusso.* . . ."

18

*E*rica snapped off the set.

She dropped her head in her hands. "Oh, God, please help," she prayed. She sat there for a moment, then ran to Alex's door and knocked.

"Yeah? Come in."

Erica pushed open the door and dropped down on a beanbag chair close to Alex's desk.

Alex looked up. "Erica! What's wrong?"

"How close are you to proving Tyson's behind our problems?"

"Why?" Alex asked. "Has something else happened?"

Erica told him what she heard on the television. "How could he know so soon, Alex? The council was meeting at the time Dad got the phone call from John Blake. Our newsman didn't even have time to call."

"I told you it was a plant. This proves it." He pulled his notebook from his pocket and grabbed a pencil. "Let's figure out the timing. Do you know exactly when the garbage is picked up?"

Erica automatically glanced at her watch. "Oh, Alex!" She jumped up. "I've got to help Paula with dinner. We'll have to work this out later. The Palmers will be here in half an hour."

"If they still come," remarked Alex. He looked down at his notebook. "You don't know when the garbage is picked up?"

"No, except it's before we get to the *Kerusso* from school. You could call their office." She dashed out the door.

Mr. Nelson arrived home minutes before the Palmers were due. Alex and Erica hurried to meet him.

"What happened, Dad?" asked Alex.

"Nothing. The plate found in the dumpster was the one used to make the posters."

"Have you been charged?" asked Erica.

"No. Only Palmer can bring charges and they've been unable to get in touch with him. He probably hasn't heard about it yet. Hopefully, he is on his way here, and we can work things out."

"There's not much chance he hasn't heard," said Erica. "Channel 5 had a story on the local news—direct coverage of the Karston City Council. Mr. Tyson accused you of libel."

"The TV stations don't usually cover city council meetings," said Mr. Nelson.

"The newscaster said they'd received a tip," said Erica. "What—"

The doorbell rang. "At least the Palmers came," said Mr. Nelson as he went to answer. "That's a good sign."

Erica started into the kitchen.

"Come in," her father invited. "I'm glad to see you."

"Take a close look, because we're not staying!" shouted Senator Palmer.

Erica stopped in the kitchen doorway. Senator Palmer's red hair flamed, and belligerence radiated from his stocky body. His wife, delicate and petite, clung to his arm, looking worriedly from her husband to Mr. Nelson.

"Come in," repeated Mr. Nelson. "Give us an opportunity to explain."

"I listened to your explanation the other day," said Senator Palmer. "And I believed you. Then tonight, what do I hear? Proof that you made the posters."

"Planted," said Alex.

"Planted?" asked Mrs. Palmer, her voice a surprising, deep contralto.

"Obvious." Alex waved an arm in the air. "Tyson has made his first slip. He—"

"That's the same kind of gobbledegook I heard from you before," Senator Palmer interrupted. "I'm not buying it this time." He glared at Mr. Nelson. "What's your story?"

"I have none," replied Mr. Nelson. "I just returned from the City Attorney's office. But I didn't make that plate."

"Of course he didn't," insisted Alex. "Compute the facts. Tyson knew too soon about the plate's being in our dumpster. Our garbage was being picked up about the time the city council meeting started. He had to have done it himself. He couldn't have found it out any other way."

"Yeah?"

"Yeah," Alex responded. "Even before that, he'd tipped off channel 5 news."

Erica again watched Senator Palmer's volatile anger fade. "Do you have an answer for everything, young man?"

"No. If I did, I'd be able to expose Tyson and wind up this whole thing."

Mrs. Palmer laughed. "I believe you. And I hope you do it soon. It's hard to live with the mercurial rages Ralph has been indulging in lately."

The Palmers allowed Mr. Nelson to take their coats and usher them into the living room. Erica went to help Paula. "The crisis is over. We still have guests for dinner," she whispered. "For a while it was touch and go."

"I heard," Paula whispered back. "Alex saved the day—again." She finished tossing the salad. "That's it," she said. "Remember, the pie is in the refrigerator. Everything's ready. I'll slip out now."

Erica reached out and touched Paula's arm. "Thanks so much. I don't know what we'd do without you."

Paula smiled. "You'd do just fine, but I'm glad I'm here to help. See you tomorrow."

———

Over dessert Palmer said, "You've convinced me that you really didn't produce that poster."

"We'd sure be crazy to put the evidence in our own garbage if we did," Alex said.

Senator Palmer laughed. "I can see that. I guess I let my temper get out of hand and didn't think straight." He balanced a small bite of pie on his fork. "But now, let's get down to cases. Why would the same person want to blacken my character and put you out of business? Or is it the same person?"

"We assume it is," said Mr. Nelson, "but, of course, we can't be sure."

"But why?" asked the senator.

"If we knew why," interjected Alex, "we'd be able to prove who's behind it."

Mr. Nelson looked determined. "I've been trying to stay low key, to convince the people of Karston, particularly the business community, that I'm above board and that the paper is valuable for advertising," he said. "But today's attack was too much. I see I need to change my tactics."

"What will you do?" asked Mrs. Palmer.

"I'm going to fight—to find out if Tyson is behind it and why. If he is, I'm going to stop him, legally, of course. I'll have to consult a lawyer to see what courses of action are open to me."

"I'm an attorney," said Senator Palmer. "I'll represent you without charge."

Erica looked at her father.

A thoughtful expression darkened his eyes. "I appreciate your offer, but I can still afford to pay."

"It's not a matter of affording," protested the senator. "I didn't mean that. I figure we're in this together. We have the same antagonist, the same battle to fight. Let's pool our resources."

Discussion followed about strategy, what charges could be brought against Tyson, if they could prove his guilt, and what steps they would each take.

Erica watched Alex. Why was he so quiet? He only listened, not offering any suggestions. Was he thinking that the adults were taking his mystery from him and that he wouldn't have the opportunity to resolve it by himself?

Erica poured another cup of coffee for the Palmers and her father. The conversation changed.

"About that editorial," said Senator Palmer. "At first I was furious. But after I read it again, Sally and I did some research. You're right. The Economy Builder Bill does benefit some, but it works a hardship on others." He reached out to grasp his wife's hand. "We've decided that regardless of what it does to my career, I'm removing my support from the bill and will actively campaign against it. Meanwhile, I'll work out something more equitable to present at the next session."

"Good," Mr. Nelson smiled. "I don't think it'll hurt your career. It may even move you up a notch or two."

"People are most important," said Mrs. Palmer. "Ralph ran for the Senate because of his strong feelings that people count and that more should be done to make the quality of life better in the state of Washington."

Finally Alex entered the conversation. "How long have you known Mr. Tyson?"

"Why, I'm not sure," responded Senator Palmer. "I guess I met him about the time I was elected to office. I remember he invited us for dinner one night." The senator's stubby fingers ran through his coppery red hair. "You know, that night was the first time I heard the concept of the Economy Builder Bill. Tyson started talking about it. He made it sound great."

"He's one who would benefit greatly by its passage," said Mr. Nelson. "As a land developer, he would really cash in if it becomes a law."

"Did you ever live in Bozeman, Montana?" Alex asked.

"I practiced law there for three years in a firm established by one of my law-school classmates."

"And you never heard of Tyson or met him before you moved here?"

"Alex!" reproved Mr. Nelson. "I think you're insulting our guest."

"But, Dad."

"Enough, son. Senator Palmer is a victim of Mr. Tyson just as we are. There's no reason for the third degree."

Alex clamped his lips together, but the look he cast at Senator Palmer was anything but friendly.

———————

The next morning, Leslie met Erica to walk to school. "I saw the news last night!" she exclaimed. "What's your dad going to do?"

"Fight. He and Senator Palmer are going to prosecute when they prove who's behind it."

"Senator Palmer? But . . . but why would he help your dad? I'd think he would hate him."

"The Palmers had dinner with us last night. They know Dad's innocent. We're joining forces."

Leslie gave Erica a quick hug. "I was afraid your dad would carry out his threat to move you to Boston."

"I'm just afraid that there'll be another note on our locker this morning. Whoever's writing them won't miss this opportunity."

They could see the square of white stand out from the drab green of the locker as they walked down the hall. A few kids stood at lockers nearby, but none looked guilty or nervous. The red-haired sophomore leaned into his locker. Carolyn was nowhere in sight.

With a resigned sigh, Erica reached for the envelope and ripped it open. The paper and typing were the same. She gasped. The note had nothing to do with Tyson's accusation about the poster. Instead it read:

Well, well. So little brother Alex is a criminal. A felon. A burglar. What did he steal? How come it wasn't in the famous *Kerusso* this week? Trying to keep it a family secret?

Anger made Erica's hands shake as she passed the note to Leslie.

"How could anyone have found out?" Leslie asked after reading the note.

Erica spread her hands in a helpless gesture. "I don't know." She took the note and jammed it into her pocket. "I hate to show this to Dad. Poor Alex. He was hoping he wouldn't disgrace Dad—especially now."

Whoever had found out did a good job of spreading the news. Throughout the day, various schoolmates would call to Erica in the halls. "Hey, what's this I hear about Alex being picked up by the cops?" or "Hear Alex's in trouble. What happened?"

When she could take no more, Erica turned swiftly and confronted the speaker. "Who told you that gossip?" she demanded.

"Are you saying it isn't true?"

"I asked you where you got your information," Erica pressed.

"It's all over school."

"Who started it?"

The answer was a shrug. She couldn't find out any more about it.

Erica was seething by the time school let out. She almost wished they *would* move to Boston.

Leslie timidly put her hand on Erica's arm. "I know this isn't the best time to ask," she said, "but would you go shopping with me tomorrow morning? I need you to help me pick out my new dress."

"Ask your mom to help," Erica said.

"Erica! You know if Mom helps, I'll get a dress suitable for a fourth grader. I want something sophisticated and glamorous. You have to help me."

Erica couldn't resist the pleading in her friend's blue eyes. It would be terrible shopping when she didn't have a date for Karlotolo, when the whole bottom had dropped out of her world. But still, Leslie was her best friend.

"Okay. I'll pick you up at nine-thirty tomorrow morning. We can be at the mall when it opens. I have an appointment with Mrs. Havig in the afternoon."

Leslie threw her arms around her friend. "Oh, thanks. I knew I could count on you."

At the newspaper office, Erica wordlessly handed the note to her father.

He looked up. "Another one?"

She nodded. "Whoever wrote this one spread the news all over school, too. At least two dozen kids gave me a hard time today."

Her father frowned as he read the note. "I wonder how they found out."

Alex came in. "What's so serious?" he asked.

Mr. Nelson gave him the note. Alex glanced at it, a smug expression sliding across his features.

"What's so funny?" demanded Erica. "I think it's terrible. Everyone knows. They're all talking about it. I thought you'd be upset."

"The kids at my school know, too," he said. "But don't you see? It's another link in Tyson's chain."

"How do you figure?" his father asked.

"We didn't tell anyone. If the police and city officials released anything, they wouldn't have used my name because I'm a minor. The only other source of information is Tyson. He's the only one who could know."

"He's right, Dad. Do you suppose Tyson is behind all the notes?"

"Maybe. But we can't jump to conclusions."

"The best thing," Alex crowed, "is that we have written proof. Everybody talking about it couldn't point to anyone special. This note might."

———

That night after the concert, Mike and Erica went to The Shack for something to eat. Brian and Leslie occupied a booth in the back. With a questioning look at Erica, Mike led the way to join them.

Over French dips and soft drinks, Erica filled them all in. "Alex is nearly jumping for joy. He thinks he can use the note to prove Tyson's involvement."

"How can he do that?" asked Brian.

"I'm not sure. But since Tyson was the only person who knew about the break-in, other than the city officials, Dad, and me, he has to be the one."

"What does your mom think about it?" asked Mike.

"Mom?" Erica stared from one friend to another. "I never even thought of Mom, not even to wish she were here. I'm sure Dad's called her by now to tell her as much as he thinks she should know." She smiled. "I think he edits a lot of the facts so she won't worry."

Later, when Mike drove up in front of Erica's house, he switched off the engine. "Brian told me he's taking Leslie to Karlotolo at the Founder's Festival," he said. "I suppose you already have a date."

"No," Erica admitted.

"Would you go with me?"

"Are you sure you should ask me?" Erica's voice was troubled.

"What do you mean?"

"Well, I . . ." Erica's voice trailed off. How could she explain without involving Carolyn?

"What is it?" prompted Mike.

"I heard that your parents were upset because you're dating me"—her voice quivered—"that people at the church are praying for you to break it off."

Mike reached out and took her hands. "That was before, Erica."

"Before what?"

"Before you accepted Christ into your life." He drew a deep breath. "The Bible says Christians aren't to be yoked with unbelievers. It can mean a lot of different things, but most Christians stress that Christians shouldn't marry non-Christians."

Erica drew back. "But we haven't even thought of marriage."

"I know. But in our society, the ultimate purpose of dating is to find a mate. And, to be honest, I discovered that I wanted to date you so much I was ready to put you before God. That's the danger. I told myself I just cared about you to lead you to Christ. I did care that way," he touched her cheek gently. "But not only that way."

Erica felt her cheeks warm. "So, since I'm a Christian now, your folks approve?"

"Of course. They both liked you a great deal the first time they met you. I think it was harder for them to counsel me against dating you than it was for me to consider not asking you out again."

"I'm glad I didn't know this before. Your mom might have thought that's why I became a Christian."

"That happens a lot. Then later the person turns his back because it wasn't real. But your spiritual growth already proves your true belief."

She smiled at him. "Then if the invitation to Karlotolo is still open, I'd love to go."

"It's a date. But first I'll see you Sunday." He jumped from the car and walked her to the porch, swinging her hand in his. At the door, he bent his head and kissed her gently on the lips. "Good night, Erica."

Happiness welled up in Erica. "Night, Mike."

19

Saturday morning, Erica pulled up in front of Leslie's home and tapped the horn.

Leslie opened the door. "Be with you in a minute."

Erica hummed while she waited. The words to the song crept into her mind: "Bind us together as only You can do." Who did she want bound together this morning? Mike and herself? She smiled, remembering his kiss.

Leslie came running down the walk and slid into the car. "Isn't it a beautiful day?" She waved her hand at the blue skies and sunshine. "Hard to believe such weather at the end of March."

"Glorious," responded Erica. "In more ways than one."

"Something's happened!" exclaimed Leslie. "You're glowing. Did you find out—?"

"No," interrupted Erica. "But we're shopping for two party dresses this morning. And I want mine to be just as sophisticated and glamorous as yours."

"Watch out, stores, here we come," crowed Leslie.

"Which mall? Everett or Alderwood?"

"Alderwood. If we don't find anything there, we can go to Everett."

"Okay, but remember, I have to be finished by noon to get to the Havigs' on time."

At Nordstrom, Leslie tried on a light pink dress that reflected its color in her cheeks and added highlights to her blond hair. She twirled in front of the mirror. "What do you think, Erica?"

"It's beautiful. The color is great."

"Is it? Are you sure pink isn't too 'little-girlish'?"

"Not that shade. And certainly not the way the dress is made."

"I hate to take the first one I try. What should I do?"

The saleslady came to her rescue. "Why don't I put it aside for a couple hours while you make up your mind?"

"Would you? Oh, that would be perfect." Leslie slipped out of the dress.

They walked through the mall. *There must be a dress just for me,* Erica thought. *One that I'll fall in love with.*

But it wasn't to be found at Lamonts.

At The Bon, Erica tried on a shimmery gray confection of a dress. It clung to her figure and draped softly.

"I think the color is wrong," Leslie said. "Not that it doesn't look good on you, but it's too old or too dull for this occasion."

Erica sighed. "I think you're right. This isn't it."

"I'd like to try this midnight blue dress," said Leslie. "It's almost the same style as the pink one at Nordstrom." She tried it on and stepped out to view herself in the three-way mirror. "What do you think?" she asked.

"Oh," Erica breathed. "It's perfect. The blue matches your eyes exactly. Oh, Les, this is the one. The pink was good, but this is terrific."

Erica glanced at her watch as she tried on a dress in burgundy. "If I don't find something here, I'll have to wait until next week."

"It's very pretty," ventured Leslie.

"But I want more than pretty," Erica said. "I want smashing. Extra special." She turned back to the dressing room. "I'm not going to find it today."

Erica drove Leslie home, then stopped to pick up her Bible, notebook, and some books she had borrowed from Mrs. Havig. Alex was in the kitchen eating a sandwich.

Erica joined him. "Where's Dad?" she asked, spreading tuna over a slice of wheat bread.

"Either at *The Kerusso* or at Palmers'. They're talking about a possible law suit and all that legal stuff."

"I'm on my way to the Havigs'," Erica said. "What are your plans for the afternoon?"

"Depends on the mail. If I get a package I'm expecting, I'll spend the afternoon here. If it doesn't come, I'm going over to Pete's." He took a big bite of his sandwich.

"You're to stay away from Tyson, remember."

"How could I forget? Dad made it very plain." He smiled impishly up at Erica. "I don't need anything more from him anyway. I wouldn't follow him even if Dad hadn't said anything."

"Okay. Take care. I should be home around four."

The aroma of freshly baked cookies greeted Erica again as she stepped into the Havig kitchen. "Do you bake every Saturday?" she asked Ellen.

"Well, with three boys and Hank, cookies don't last long. I made chocolate with chocolate frosting today. Sound good?"

"Delicious. May I pour the milk?"

"The glasses are there." Ellen nodded toward the cupboard to the right of the sink. "How did your week go?"

"Oh!" exclaimed Erica. "God is answering one of our prayers already."

"Which one? Tell me." Ellen put a plate of warm cookies on the table between them and sat down.

Erica explained about the notes, especially the latest one about Alex and the burglary. She went on to tell about Tyson's public accusation of her father and the evidence planted in the dumpster.

"Well, God's answer can't be in resolving the problems at *The Kerusso*. What is it?"

Erica smiled. "It may be. According to Alex, all of this adds to the proof that Tyson is really behind everything. But the real answer is in my attitude toward Mom. I didn't once think, 'She should be here.' It surprised me when Mike asked me what she thought of it all."

"What was your response then?"

"I just told him Dad had probably called, editing what he told her to spare her worry. I felt glad he was protecting her."

"Good girl. God will continue to win the victory for you if you let Him."

"It is a victory. I recognize that, but I still don't think a mother should put her career first, not when it takes the total commitment Mom has."

"In most instances, I agree with you. Mainly because God asks that we give Him our total commitment. We can't give it in two places. I've found that the only way life works is if I put God first, family second, and job third."

"God first, family second, job third," Erica repeated. "That's the way I feel. Of course, until a couple of weeks ago, I didn't know about putting God first."

"That's most important. When God is first, He puts every other area of our lives into perspective."

"So, if we put God first, then we'll know how to live the way we should, the way He wants us to."

"Right," agreed Ellen. "And part of putting Him first is learning about Him. That's why our daily quiet time is so important. How did you do this week?"

"Much better. I want to tell you some of the things I learned and ask some questions."

As they enjoyed their chocolate cookies and milk, Ellen and Erica opened their Bibles and notebooks.

They had just finished with prayer when a commotion began outside. The kitchen door flew open and Mike entered, followed by Geoff, Wayne, Alex, and Pete.

Mike sniffed. "Good. I bribed Alex and Pete with freshly baked cookies. I'd hate to disappoint them." He introduced Pete to his mother.

While she heaped a plate with cookies, Erica got glasses from the cupboard and poured milk for everyone. Cookies and milk disappeared amidst much laughter and chatter.

After a while, Erica gathered up her books. "Alex, I think we'd better head for home," she said. "Dad will be wondering where we are. Come on, Pete."

On the way home, Alex said, "This afternoon I saw that awful black-haired girl Mike's been taking to church."

"Oh?" questioned Erica. "Carolyn?"

"Yeah. She was hanging on Jinson's arm. She was all gussied

up, with high heels, smears of makeup, and her hair fixed funny."

Knowing Alex, Erica felt he might be exaggerating a bit. "She has the right to get dressed up and date whomever she wants."

"But the guy is one of Tyson's men."

"How do you know?"

Alex shrugged. "Do you think I just fell off a turnip truck? I followed Tyson for weeks. I've seen this guy with him. He runs Tyson's errands, drives his car."

"Carolyn's free to date."

"Aw, you don't get it. She's hand in glove with Tyson's bunch. That means she's against us. But I'll bet she's so dumb she doesn't know what's really happening."

Erica glanced at her brother. The look on his face told her he wasn't being derogatory. He really felt Carolyn didn't know the kind of people she was dealing with.

Pete piped up from the backseat. "Mike was with us when we saw her. He said he'd find some way to help her."

Erica looked at Pete in the rearview mirror. "Sounds like Mike. Maybe she does need help." In her heart Erica couldn't believe that Carolyn was that naive. The way she acted, she knew the score. "That would explain how she always knows what's going on," she said aloud. "She always has some remark about whatever happens to us or at the paper."

Alex grunted. "You still don't understand. It makes her the prime suspect for the notes. She's always been a possibility, but this makes it almost sure."

Erica thought about it. "Yes, she could be doing it. But I haven't ruled out that red-haired kid whose locker is close to mine. He's always there. He never smiles. He pretends to ignore me, but I think he's watching me."

"Why don't you find out who he is? If we know his name, we can see if he has a reason to harass us."

"How do I find out?"

"Ask him," suggested Pete.

"Or ask someone who has a locker near him," Alex said. "You could even walk behind him and see if his name is on his notebook or whatever. Don't be so dumb, Erica."

"All right, Alex," Erica replied. "I'll find out Monday."

The next day, Alex accompanied Mike and Erica to church. They stopped at Carolyn's house. Erica watched as Carolyn slid into the backseat, a frown marring her perfect complexion and regular features. "Oh, do I sit with the little criminal?"

A disgusted look crept across Alex's face. He turned his back and stared out the window. He wouldn't say a word, not even to Mike.

Again Carolyn managed to sit in the front seat on the way home, insisting that Mike take the Nelsons home first. When Mike dropped them off, he jumped out of the car. With one arm across Alex's shoulder and the other around Erica's waist, he walked them to the door. "I'll call you later, Erica," he said with a smile.

"We're going to the Palmers' for dinner this afternoon. But I should be home in time to go to church tonight. If I am, I'll see you there."

"Okay. Have a nice afternoon." His voice dropped. "Oh, and pray, would you? I want to find out if Carolyn knows she's keeping bad company. I'd like to help her if I can."

Erica nodded, but her heart twisted with anger as she saw Carolyn lean toward Mike, closing the space between them as they drove off.

———

That afternoon, the Palmers greeted them warmly and ushered them into the living room. Erica admired the frilly pink apron Mrs. Palmer wore over her lavender dress.

"Excuse me," said Mrs. Palmer. "I'll slip into the kitchen and put the finishing touches on dinner. It will be ready soon."

"May I help?" Erica asked.

"No, that's all right. I'll only be a minute."

Erica sank into a deep chair and looked around the room. Its elegance spoke of an emphasis on entertaining rather than on hominess. A cold sparseness characterized the room. There was no lack of furnishings. It just wasn't cozy.

Alex was quiet, busily taking notes as he listened intently to the conversation between his father and Senator Palmer.

Mrs. Palmer came to the doorway. "We're ready to eat. Ralph, would you call Jerry?"

The Nelsons followed Mrs. Palmer into the dining room while Senator Palmer knocked at a door down the hallway. "Time to eat, Jerry. Come along."

A mumble came through the door.

"Jerry! Now! Your mother has everything on the table."

Senator Palmer rejoined them. "Jerry's working on a school project he doesn't want to leave. He'll be right here."

Mrs. Palmer fidgeted with her napkin. Alex watched the door expectantly. It swung open. Erica's eyes widened in amazement. She looked from the boy's red hair to the flaming crown of his father and wondered why she hadn't made the connection before.

Her eyes met Alex's across the table. She nodded in answer to the question on his face.

"This is our son, Jerry," Senator Palmer said. "Jerry, Mr. Nelson."

Mr. Nelson reached out to shake hands, but Jerry turned and walked around to the other side of the table.

"And you may know Erica or Alex."

Alex shook his head, saying, "Hi. How are you?"

Erica swallowed with difficulty. "I'm glad to meet you," she said. "I've seen you in the hall at school but didn't know who you were."

Jerry scowled and mumbled something that sounded like, "So what?"

Senator Palmer frowned at his son, but Jerry didn't notice. He looked at no one. He kept his eyes on his plate throughout the whole meal and excused himself as soon as his parents would let him go.

Alex was ready to burst by the time they got into their car to leave. "I'll bet he's the one," he said.

"One what?" asked Mr. Nelson.

"The note-writer. Dad, he's the red-haired boy who has a

locker close to Erica's. He's always there. Erica kept wondering, but we were all so sure Carolyn did it, I didn't consider him." He looked with disgust at Erica. "And, of course, she didn't bother to find out who he was."

"Hey, slow down, son. It's obvious we aren't his favorite people, but that doesn't make him guilty of the notes."

"No. But it makes him a prime suspect."

Erica nodded thoughtfully. "You know, I can understand how he feels. It's the same way I feel about Tyson, who I think is hurting Dad. He must think we're out to do harm to Senator Palmer, so naturally he'd hate us."

"But we're not," reasoned Alex.

"But he isn't sure of that, even now. For all he knows, we could be faking."

"Good perception, Erica," her father said.

———

Monday afternoon, Erica dashed into *The Kerusso* office to finish her weekly column. The old atmosphere of bustling activity pervaded the office.

She stopped by the ad desk. "What's going on?" she asked.

The ad man looked up from the layout he was working on and grinned. "We sold some ads today. I sold seven and Fred sold fourteen. Just in time for the Karston Founder's Festival splurge. How's that for success?"

"Great. Why did they change their minds?"

His grin widened. "I think it has a lot to do with your dad and Senator Palmer joining forces. And it probably didn't hurt for Mrs. Palmer to tell various merchants that she missed seeing their ads in *The Kerusso* and that she'd like to know about their specials before she got to the store."

"I can see her doing that," Erica laughed. "Bless her. I hope the trend continues." She walked over to her desk.

Alex flung open the door, pulling an older man into the room with him. "Where's Dad?" he called. "Is he in his office?"

The receptionist looked up with a smile. "Not at the moment. He should be back soon."

Alex grinned his cocky grin. "Thanks. We'll wait." He turned to the man. "C'mon. We'll talk to my sister until Dad gets back."

Alex tugged at the man's sleeve, and he shuffled after him.

The old man moved uncertainly. His eyes shot fearful, darting glances all around the office.

"This is Milton Glass," Alex said, pulling him to a stop by Erica's desk. "Milton makes part of his living by putting up posters."

The old man twisted his hands together. "Milton don't do nothin' wrong. Just what he gets paid to do."

"That's right, Milton," reassured Alex. "We don't think you did anything wrong. I just hope you can help us solve a mystery."

Milton's eyes brightened. "A mystery? Milton loves mysteries, like Perry Mason on TV."

Erica glanced at Alex. At his nod, she said, "We have our own mystery. Would you like to help us find out who the villain is?"

"Did he murder someone?" asked Milton.

"No. But he's trying to ruin one man's reputation and take business away from others. He's breaking the law and hurting people. We'd like to stop him."

Milton's fingers relaxed, and his eyes stopped their relentless movement, focusing on Erica. "Milton likes to help. What can he do?"

"Do you have a copy of the Palmer poster, Erica?" asked Alex. "I'd like to show it to Milton."

"It's in Dad's office." She jumped up and went to get it.

Milton's eyes followed her. "She's a right pretty girl. Milton likes her. He wants to help her."

Erica came back, holding the poster so Milton could see.

"Do you remember this one?" Alex asked gently.

Milton squinted at it. His head bobbed up and down. "Sure do. Got paid good for that one. More than any other."

"Who paid you?" asked Alex.

A dullness dropped over Milton's eyes. "I don't know as Milton should tell that. Don't want no more to do with it."

Erica touched his arm, her eyes pleading with his. "Please, it's important. The poster has hurt a lot of people. It's the center of our mystery. If you can tell us who paid you to put it up, we can make everything right."

Milton looked at Erica, the battle evident in his face. "He told me not to tell. He say Milton get in trouble if I tell."

Erica looked sympathetically at the old man. "We don't want you to get—"

"Tell you what," interrupted Alex. "If you tell us, we'll keep it a secret until the bad guy goes to jail and can't hurt you. Then we'll be able to solve our mystery, and you'll be safe."

Milton walked around the desk to stand close to Erica. Alex followed.

"Is it safe to talk here?" Milton asked. His eyes began to dart around the room again, not missing anything.

"Sure it's safe. I guarantee it," Alex said. "No one can hear us."

With one last encompassing glance, Milton leaned close to Erica and Alex and whispered. "It was Mr. Nelson—the guy that owns this paper."

20

"No!" Erica gasped, her hand rising to her throat.

"That can't be!" exclaimed Alex. "I know it wasn't."

Milton's head bobbed vigorously. "Yup. That's who it was. He told me. Told me his name was Nelson. Told me he ran the paper. Milton don't forget."

Erica looked hopelessly at Alex. "Do you suppose. . . ?"

"Did I help? Milton wants to help." He looked anxiously from one to the other.

"You tried," soothed Erica. "You tried, but we can't believe it was Mr. Nelson who paid you to put up the posters."

Hurt filled Milton's eyes. "Milton don't lie," he protested. "I tell the truth."

"Are my kids saying you don't tell the truth?" asked Mr. Nelson, coming up behind Milton.

Milton jumped. His eyes darted here and there, swiftly at Mr. Nelson's face, then away, around the room, then at Erica and Alex.

Erica watched him. She saw no recognition. "Milton," she asked, "would you know Mr. Nelson again if you saw him?"

Once again his head bobbed. "Never forget a face. I'd remember. Remember well." His hands twisted in agonized motion.

Erica touched his hands lightly. "Milton, look at this man." She pointed to her father. "Do you know him?"

Head bobbing, Milton said, "Yes and no. I don't know his name, but he's nice. He always smiles at me when we meet."

Very gently, Erica said, "This is Richard Nelson. He's my father, and he owns and publishes the paper."

"No," Milton denied. He shook his head vigorously. "Mr. Nel-

165

son is gray. He has a beard. Here, I show you." Milton picked up a pad and pencil from Erica's desk. With a few strokes, a face emerged on the paper. Tyson. Unmistakably Tyson.

"Thank you, Milton. That's wonderful. You are an exceptional artist." Erica took the picture. "This is very good."

Pleasure wreathed Milton's face. "Did Milton help? Will you solve your mystery?"

"Oh yes. You've been a big help."

"I'll call Senator Palmer and tell him," said Mr. Nelson, moving toward his office.

Fright etched Milton's face. He turned to Erica. "You promised."

"Dad," Alex said, "you can't do that. We gave Milton our word we wouldn't tell anyone what he told us until the bad guy is in police custody."

"But—" started Mr. Nelson.

"Dad, we promised," added Erica. "Tyson threatened Milton. We have to protect him."

"Besides, Dad, if we let this slip now, Tyson may get away. It would be better to keep it until we have all our proof and can nail him with everything at once."

Mr. Nelson nodded. "Okay. I won't ask you to break your word." He turned to Milton. "Thank you, Milton. We owe you a great deal. I appreciate your risking your safety for us."

Tears glistened in Milton's eyes as he turned to go. He shuffled through the room to the door, then turned to wave goodbye.

Alex and Erica followed their father into his office. Alex laid Milton's drawing on the desk.

"Our first tangible proof that Tyson is involved," he crowed. "I told you I'd have proof within a month, and here it is."

Mr. Nelson hesitated. "It appears to be, son, but there are a couple of hitches. The first is Milton himself. Many people would not consider his testimony valid."

"Why not?" Erica asked. She picked up the drawing and studied it. "This is excellent. How could anyone doubt who it is?"

"Oh, the drawing is recognizable, all right," her father said, leaning back in his chair, stretching out his feet in front of him. "It's just that some people may not think Milton is capable of intelligent observations."

"Not capable?" Alex shouted, banging his fist on a pile of page proofs. "He's probably more observant than half this town put together."

"True, but the fact remains that people may not accept his word," his father contended.

"But the sketch proves that Tyson, not you, wanted to smear Palmer," Erica insisted.

Her father nodded. "Yes, and I wish I knew why."

"I think I know," said Alex with a secretive smile. "But I'm waiting for proof on that, too."

"Are you looking for the office that printed the poster?" asked Erica.

"No. Too many places have the capability, and no one's going to admit it. Besides, the plate was planted in our dumpster, so it's not likely we'd find any evidence lying around to convict the real printer."

"The roughs might be," said Mr. Nelson. "Or a contract between the printer and whoever paid for them. But," he hastened to add, "I don't want you looking for them."

Alex shook his head. "I did think about the paste-ups for that poster, but they've probably been destroyed. Besides, if I'm right about Tyson's motive, then we won't need the printer."

"Okay, son. Keep at it, without bugging Tyson. Now, to current events. Did you hear about the advertisers who bought this week?"

"It must penetrate even the densest of minds that if Palmer doesn't believe you smeared him, they shouldn't believe it either," Alex said. "But people are really dumb."

Mr. Nelson smiled. "Oh, come on, Alex. They just don't take time to think. And speaking of time, we're at deadline for articles. What's your column about this week, Erica? Is it ready?"

Erica jumped up. "Give me five minutes for the final typing. It's about spring vacation."

"Spring vacation? When is it?"

"Next week."

"Oh. I was going to send you and Alex to Boston for the week. You could visit your mother and see the sights."

"Dad! I couldn't go to Boston now," protested Alex. "Things are coming to a head, and I can't be gone. I want to be here for the arrest."

"I'd just as soon stay, too, Dad. I need to do some shopping. I haven't found a dress for Karlotolo yet. Besides, with advertisers coming back, we'll be busy again."

Mr. Nelson picked up a sheaf of dummies. "All right," he said. "Perhaps we can all go after school is out."

The highlight of spring vacation was a shopping trip with Leslie. At a small specialty shop in Everett, Erica found the perfect dress. Its vibrant red color complemented her complexion and the style enhanced her figure. She found a matching evening bag and shoes.

Leslie purchased a pair of shoes. "Oh, I wish it were time for Karlotolo," she wailed. "I can't wait for us to wear our beautiful dresses."

"It's only a couple weeks," said Erica. "In the meantime, occupy your mind by doing something interesting."

"Like what?" Leslie demanded. "What could be that exciting?"

"Well, next Tuesday is Brian's birthday. You could plan a celebration."

"Next Tuesday? Oh, Erica. Why didn't you tell me sooner? How can I plan a party that fast?"

Erica grinned. "I'm sure you'll come up with something."

"Should we make it a big party or just a small one?" Leslie said, almost to herself. "What would Brian like best? Should we—oh, I know. Erica, let's make it just the four of us—you and Mike, Brian and me. We'll go down to the Aquarium, and the Omnidome, and then have dinner at the Spaghetti Warehouse."

"He'd like that."

Leslie threw her arms around Erica. "Perfect! But," she hesitated, "I'd kind of like it to be a surprise. Can we do it?"

They discussed various plans and finally decided that Erica would invite Brian to her house. Mike and Leslie would just happen to drop in.

"Now," said Leslie. "I've got to find him a present. What should I get him? Are you going to buy something?"

"Oh, I already have his gift," smiled Erica. "I bought it a couple of weeks ago."

"What is it?"

"I'm not telling. But I'll help you shop."

They spent the afternoon going from store to store. Leslie took turns being excited and depressed as she came up with and discarded idea after idea. Finally she chose an extravagant laser-designed desk appointment calendar. "If he's going to be an executive someday, he'll need something like this," she said.

———

Brian's birthday evening started off as they planned. He was completely surprised and thoroughly enjoyed the Aquarium. At the Omnidome they saw an updated version of "Eruption of Mount St. Helens," which showed the aftereffects of the 1980 eruption.

When they finished their meal at the Spaghetti Warehouse, Leslie placed a beautifully gift-wrapped box beside Brian's plate. Mike and Erica each produced cards and laid them on the table.

Brian looked from one to another with a pleased but almost embarrassed look on his face. "Hey, you didn't have to do this. The Aquarium and dinner were enough."

He picked up Mike's card first, opened and read it. "Thanks," he said. As he pulled Erica's card from its envelope, something dropped out. He bent to pick it up.

"All right! Two tickets to the Garth Brooks concert next month. Les, we've got a date. You free on the fourteenth?"

"Sure am. Wouldn't miss it for anything."

"Thanks, Erica. You always know just the gift to please. Good seats, too." He leaned over and pecked her on the cheek. "You're a real pal."

As Brian started unwrapping Leslie's gift, a brittle voice from behind Erica said, "Mind if I join the party?"

Mike got up. "Please do." He spotted an empty chair and pulled it over to their table.

"Hi, birthday boy," Carolyn cooed, her syrupy voice causing chills to wiggle down Erica's back.

"Hi," said Brian. "Here alone?"

Carolyn shook her head. "Well, yes. I . . . came with someone I don't want to go home with." She turned a sweet smile on Mike. "When I saw Mike, I knew he'd be glad to give me a ride, so I walked out on the jerk."

Erica fought against the anger demanding to be vented on Carolyn. *Lord,* she prayed silently, *Mike is trying to win her for you. Don't let me ruin it.*

"We'll be glad to have you ride home with us," she said. "After Brian opens his present, we'll go."

"Oh, don't rush on my account. Mom won't expect me for another couple of hours," Carolyn said. And then, in an almost inaudible voice, she added, "If then."

Sympathy melted the anger in Erica's heart. Could it be that Carolyn's mother cared less than her own mother did? Aloud she said, "But we need to get home. School tomorrow."

Brian opened Leslie's gift and told her how much he liked it, but somehow the sparkle had gone out of the evening. It was an unusually silent group that trouped out to the car.

Mike dropped Leslie off first, then drove to Erica's home. Brian jumped out and opened Erica's door with a flourish. "Fair Maiden, may I escort you?" He bowed.

Erica slid out of the car. "Thanks for a lovely evening, Mike. See you tomorrow, Carolyn."

Carolyn waved as Mike drove off.

Brian started walking with Erica to her front door. "Is that the girl who's been leaving the notes?" he asked.

"Well," Erica said, "she's my guess, although Senator Palmer's son is a close second. Either one could be doing it."

"It's obvious she doesn't like you very much," said Brian. "Whatever her reason, her hate might be a strong enough motive."

Erica felt troubled. "I . . . I guess so. I've thought of her as guilty for so long, it's difficult to think clearly about her. But tonight I began to feel sorry for her. Her mother must not care much about her."

"It didn't sound like it, did it?" Brian agreed as they reached the door. "Well, good night, Erica. Right now, I've got to cram, then hit the sack. Thanks again for the Garth Brooks tickets."

———

Saturday morning, as Erica worked in the den, struggling to cut her weekly column to size, the doorbell rang. She started to get up but heard Alex tearing for the door. She smiled and picked up her pencil again.

"I have a package for Alex Nelson," a deep voice boomed. "Will you sign on line twelve?"

"Sure," replied Alex.

There was a brief silence.

"The box is heavy. Want me to wheel it inside?" the voice came again.

"Yeah. Put it right over there."

A thud shook the floor, the door slammed, and then Alex gave a victorious yelp.

Her curiosity aroused, Erica stepped into the hall. "What did you get?"

Alex looked up from tearing open the box. "Uh, nothing."

"A big box for nothing?" she responded.

"It's private, okay?"

"Is it something about Tyson?"

"Uh, maybe. Look, help me carry it down to my room and I'll give you a hint. But you have to keep it to yourself."

"Okay." Erica stooped and helped Alex pick up the box. It was heavy. Very heavy. They struggled down the stairs and into Alex's room.

"Fine," Alex grunted. "Let's put it in the corner."

They maneuvered it to where Alex designated and then stood up straight.

"Whew," Erica groaned, "some box. Now my hint."

Alex grinned. "Bribery works every time. Now that the box is—"

"Alex!" Erica threatened, laughter gleaming in her eyes. "You have to keep your word."

"Okay, okay. It may be nothing, like I said upstairs, but it may be proof."

"About Tyson?"

"Possibly. I have to search through it."

"What is it?"

"Can't tell you. You have your hint—well, more than a hint. That's all I'm saying. Now, go away. I have work to do."

"Want help?"

"Maybe, from Pete."

Erica gave up. "You win. I'm going to fix lunch. Will you have time to eat?"

"Always," Alex smiled impishly at his sister. "You know that."

———

The next morning, when Erica started getting ready for church, her hand caressed the silky fabric of the red party dress. She nestled the rich folds to her cheek. "Friday night I get to wear you," she breathed. Laughing at herself, she pulled out a navy blue two-piece dress and quickly slipped into it. She touched her lips with rosy gloss, then walked out to knock on Alex's door.

"Are you going with me?" she called.

"No. I'm busy with this . . . uh, this work I'm doing. It's taking longer than I thought. See you later."

Erica ran up the stairs, laid her Bible and purse on a table near the door, and stuck her head in the den. "I'll be off in just a few minutes, Dad. Mike's picking me up. See you after church, unless you'd like to go, too."

Her father looked up. "Maybe if I'd gotten the invitation a bit sooner." He looked down at his worn Dockers and faded sweater. "I'm hardly dressed for church."

"Lots of people go that way. Jeans, flannel shirts and stuff."

"Well, I'd feel underdressed."

"Then I'll ask you now for next week. Okay?"

"I'll plan on it."

The doorbell rang. Erica ran to answer. Her father came to the door behind her.

Erica pulled the door wide. "Hi, Mike."

"Hi. Hello, Mr. Nelson. How are you this morning?"

"Fine, thanks."

Mike looked around. "Isn't Alex coming today?"

"No," said Erica. "He's all wrapped up in a box full of something he said is nothing, but that nothing is something that's taking all his time."

Mike laughed. "Would you like to repeat that?"

"I don't think she could," said Mr. Nelson. "But I understand what she means. He won't come out of his room except for food."

"That's the second passenger who's deserted me this morning. You wouldn't like to come along to fill up the empty space, would you, sir?"

Erica's father made a deprecating sweep of his hand over his old clothes. "Erica asked me a couple of minutes ago. I told her I'd go next week. I'm not exactly dressed for it today."

"Umm. Easter Sunday. Good. I'll look forward to taking you then."

"That's a good day to start back to church."

Erica looked quizzically at her father. Did he mean it? Was he really thinking of going regularly—not just a one-time thing?

Mike broke into her thoughts. "Well, Erica, we'd better go. See you later, Mr. Nelson."

"Bye, Dad." Erica reached up to kiss her father's cheek. "Be home right after church."

He gave her a light push toward the door. "Only if you get there in the first place."

She laughed. "I'm going. Watch out for the cloud of dust."

———

The Saturday of the Karston Founder's Festival, Erica watched the parade, excitedly waiting to see Leslie march past. After Leslie changed from her band uniform, they drove to the airport for the air show.

Mike and Brian joined the girls to watch four small planes imitating the formations of the Blue Angels. An old biplane did rolls, lazy eights, and other barnstorming aerobatics.

Erica skipped the horse show and went home to take a long bath with scented bath oil. After giving herself a facial and manicuring her nails, she spent a long time applying her makeup so that it was perfect.

She tried out a new sweeping hair style but combed it out in disgust. *Mike likes it loose,* she thought. She let it flow to her shoulders, catching the glow of her dressing lamp.

At last it was time to slip into the silky red dress. Paula came down to help. Erica felt a small twinge of regret, wishing her mother could be there. She shrugged it away and smiled at Paula.

Together they stood in front of the full-length mirror. Paula tugged lightly on the dress here and there until it settled perfectly over Erica's tall, slim figure. "There!" she said. "You look absolutely beautiful."

Erica gave her an impulsive hug. "Thank you. Do you think I should wear jewelry? I was considering this gold chain."

"Let's see." Paula picked up the chain and fastened it at Erica's neck. She stood back, squinted her eyes a bit, and studied Erica's reflection. She nodded. "Just right. Do you have a gold bracelet to wear?"

Erica pulled open a small drawer in her dressing table. A small selection of bracelets lay on the velveteen lining. Paula picked up a wide gold band. "This one would be perfect."

Erica slipped it on. She smiled at her reflection. "You're right. It adds exactly the right touch. Thank you, Paula."

As they walked up the stairs together, Erica nearly floated with excitement. When she stepped into the den, Mr. Nelson's eyes widened in delight.

"Do I look all right?" Erica asked.

"All right? No." He stood slowly to his feet. "You're much more than all right. You're beautiful." Gently, he held her by the shoulders and kissed her forehead. "You're so beautiful, I'm not sure I should let you go out with that young man of yours."

Erica returned his kiss. "I'll dump him if you'd be my date," she giggled.

He smiled tenderly down at her. "That's a tempting offer, but I don't think I could be that cruel."

Alex stampeded into the room. "I thought dinner was ready. . . . Wow! Is that my sister? You look fantastic, Erica, except you've got too much gunk on your face."

Erica turned to her father, eyebrow quirked in concern.

"He's too young to appreciate the role of makeup in a woman's life," her father assured her. "You look perfect."

"Aw, she's okay," Alex admitted. "How about dinner?"

Erica reached out and ruffled his hair. "Don't you think of anything but food?"

"Sure. I've been spending long hours of drudgery over the tr— the stuff in my room."

"Making progress?" Erica asked.

"Well, I'm getting through it, but it's not giving me the information I'd hoped for. I haven't given up yet though."

The doorbell rang. Alex answered it and brought Mike into the den.

Erica drew a quick breath. Mike looked more handsome than she had ever seen him. The crisp whiteness of his shirt contrasted against the ink navy of his suit. His eyes sparkled with admiration for Erica as he held out a florist's box.

"The lady at the shop assured me this would be perfect with a red dress. I hope she's right."

Erica opened it and drew out a corsage of tiny white rosebuds with red tips, framed in a mass of delicate baby's breath. "It's beautiful," she breathed. "Here, Dad, would you?"

He pinned it in place, then turned her to face Mike. "There. For one evening I loan you the prettiest girl of Karston."

Erica felt color warm her cheeks. Pride swelled within her that her father cared so much. Impulsively, she turned and hugged him tight.

"Careful, Erica," he whispered in her ear. "You don't want to crush your flowers. Have a good time."

Hand in hand, she and Mike left the house and got into his car. Brian dashed across the lawn with a florist box tucked under his arm, struggling to tie his tie as he ran.

As they drove to pick up Leslie, Erica's heart overflowed with happiness. When Brian finally straightened his tie, he looked almost as great as Mike. *How super to have such great friends as these,* she thought.

The foyer of the new high-school auditorium became a kaleidoscope of vibrant color as couples mingled and chatted before going inside to find their seats.

The quality and variety of acts for the show were better than ever—everything from a lyric soprano to four young men pantomiming country songs, from a stand-up comic to clowns and a tumbling act.

As a grand finale, the orchestra began playing what was traditionally the last musical number, a piece composed for the first Karlotolo. The audience stood and sang as the words were flashed on giant screens. They continued to stand, and everyone applauded as the players came out for one last bow and the final chorus of Karlotolo's song.

Then the crowd emerged slowly from the auditorium, down the wide hall to the gymnasium.

Erica drew in a deep breath of pleasure as she and Mike stepped through the wide doors. Creative booths decorated with a myriad of blue, green, and yellow streamers had transformed the gym from a sports arena into a storybook market and carnival.

Hidden somewhere behind the streamers, an orchestra set the mood with fast-paced music. A clown with an enormous red nose and oversized white hands danced through the crowd. He stopped now and then to admire a beautiful lady, running away with exaggerated fear if her escort frowned.

Most of the people headed for the food booths strung along one side of the gym.

Mike squeezed Erica's hand. "Do you want anything to eat now?"

"Later," Erica said. "Let's see what else there is."

The two wandered up and down the "streets" of the fantasy village. Some booths displayed paintings, photographs, or sculpture. Some offered educational material or souvenirs of the festival. Others had games to raise money for various Karston projects.

Brian and Leslie caught up with them at the Historical Society booth. Mike kept trying to toss a rubber ring over the neck of a bottle, but every one bounced off.

"Here, let me try." Brian dug a quarter out of his pocket and picked up the first ring. Plop. It settled down over the bottle.

"Hey, all right!" Mike applauded.

"Do it again, Brian," urged Leslie.

Brian picked up the second ring and the third. Both followed the first, nestling over the bottle.

"That's my pal," crowed Erica. "It reminds me of all those games of horseshoes you used to win."

Brian laughed and pretended to polish his fingernails on his suit coat. "Just takes a keen eye," he bragged.

Brian accepted his prize—a miniature antique school bell—and presented it to Leslie, bowing gallantly.

Erica felt a twinge of jealousy. Brian's winnings had always been hers before.

The feeling vanished as Mike's hand dropped to her shoulder. "Look. There's one of those instant portrait booths. Let's."

"What a great souvenir," Erica agreed.

Mike and Erica stepped in front of the photographer's backdrop. Mike pulled Erica in front of him, resting his chin on her head.

The photographer cocked his head at them. "You're too dead center," he said. "Move her a little to your left. Ah, that's better."

In a couple of minutes he handed Mike the picture and an envelope. "You're a great-looking couple," he winked.

Erica studied the picture with Mike and secretly agreed with the photographer. She slipped the photo into the envelope, then she and Mike began wandering through the booths again. Before they knew it, the gymnasium lights began to blink, warning the crowd it was time to leave.

Mike started to guide Erica to the door but took her off to the side for a moment. He leaned close and spoke next to her ear. "It's been a super night. Have you enjoyed it as much as I have?"

Erica smiled up at him. "It's been wonderful. Thank you for bringing me."

"You're very special, Erica. I want you to know that, in case we don't get another chance to talk privately this evening."

"There are certain drawbacks to double dating," she said with a twinkle in her eye.

He nodded. "But some advantages, too."

When they had found Brian and Leslie, they drove to The Shack. After about an hour of snacking, chatter, and laughter, they reluctantly decided it was time to head for home.

Brian whispered something in Mike's ear. Mike grinned and nodded. "Good idea," he said.

Erica snuggled into the car seat. She was surprised when Mike headed for Leslie's home instead of hers. Her heart skipped a beat.

At Leslie's, Brian helped Leslie from the car, then waved. Mike drove off.

"What about Brian?" Erica asked.

"He wanted to be left at Leslie's. He said he could walk home. He didn't want to be hurried in saying good-night . . . and neither do I."

Mike reached over and took her hand. Erica's fingers tightened and clung to his.

"It's been the nicest evening of my life," she said. "The only way it could have been better—no, I won't even follow that thought. It's perfect."

Mike pulled up in front of her house. "It was great." He reached out and took her other hand. "Your father was right. I had the prettiest girl at Karlotolo. But since he only loaned you to me for the evening, I'd better return you now."

Helping her from the car, he walked with her to the porch. Silently, he slipped his arms around her and pulled her close, kissing her tenderly.

Erica's hand crept up to his neck and held him briefly as she returned his kiss. "Thanks, Mike." She opened the front door. "Thanks for a perfect evening," she whispered.

21

*E*aster Sunday morning, Erica sat proudly between her father and Mike, remembering her mother's phone call that morning.

Erica had tried to tell her mother about Karlotolo but sensed a lack of interest and fell silent.

In that silence, her father spoke. "We're all going to church this morning," he said. "It's Easter, a good time to start back."

"Oh." Mrs. Nelson's voice was flat. "That's very nice." She laughed. "I didn't even think about it being Easter. I have a briefcase full of work to get done today."

"We'll be thinking of you," her father said. "Don't work too hard."

"Don't you get too religious," she retorted.

Erica winced.

"Can anyone?" her father replied. "I've been reading my Bible again since Erica told me she'd invited Christ into her life. I'm finding I have a long way to go to meet minimum standards, but I'm on my way."

The silence on the other end of the line sharply contrasted the joy Erica felt.

"You'll be home next weekend?" her father asked.

"Yes, I'm planning on it."

"Oh, Mom," interrupted Erica. "Couldn't you make it the following weekend instead? May seventh is the Mothers' Tea for seniors' moms, remember? I'd like you to be here."

"May seventh?" Mrs. Nelson repeated. "I'll check my schedule."

Erica was jerked from her reverie when the song leader asked the congregation to stand. Erica stood and joined in the song of praise. She liked the way her voice blended with Mike's baritone and her father's deep bass. The harmony lent additional meaning to their worship.

After the service, Bud Norris grabbed Mr. Nelson by the shoulder and shook his hand. "It's good to see you here, Richard. I want to introduce you to a couple of people."

With a wink at Erica, her father followed Bud to a group of men. Erica watched for a moment, then felt a touch on her arm. She turned. "Hi, Becky. Wasn't that a great service?"

Becky nodded, her normal sparkle subdued by a troubled frown.

Erica reached out to her new friend. "Is something wrong?" she asked. "Is there something I can do?"

"I don't know." Becky looked at Erica as though trying to see right through her and discover what might be inside. "I'm not sure, but I've got to ask you."

"What is it?" Erica asked anxiously.

"I . . . I can't tell you now. Can I meet you somewhere this afternoon?"

"Sure. I can get the car and pick you up."

Relief flooded Becky's face. "That would be great. Would three o'clock be too early?"

"That's fine. Give me your address and I'll see you then."

Becky scribbled on a piece of paper and handed it to Erica just as Carolyn came up to join them. "There," said Becky. "I'm sure you'll find that reference helpful."

"Thanks," Erica said. "Hi, Carolyn. Did you enjoy the service?" She reached to touch Carolyn's arm.

Carolyn jerked away. She scowled at Erica. "Can't you leave me alone?"

Erica pulled back. "I didn't—"

"It's okay, Erica," Becky interrupted. "Let's go, Carolyn. Mom will be expecting me to help with Easter dinner." Becky and Carolyn walked out of the church.

Mike joined Erica at the door. "Problems?"

"I don't know. Becky wants to see me this afternoon without Carolyn knowing."

"If I can help, let me know." He smiled as Mr. Nelson came toward them. "Now that your dad's ready, shall we be on our way? Alex is already outside waiting."

———

A few minutes before three, Erica leaned into the den. "Dad, it's time for me to meet Becky. I'll be home in time to help with dinner."

Her father looked up from the papers spread on his desk. "Fine," he said absently. "Have a good time."

A war whoop echoed up the stairs, followed by thumping feet, and then by Alex himself. He burst into the room, hopping up and down with his hands raised over his head.

"What's up?" his dad asked.

"I found it. I found it. Proof against Tyson."

"Oh, Alex!" Erica cried. "I have to leave now. Can't you wait to tell until I get back?"

"Wait?" Alex looked at his dad and back to Erica. "I'm bursting!"

"Look, son, we'll want Palmer to hear this, and your friend Pete has a right to be in on it, doesn't he?"

"Yeah, he'll want to know."

"How about getting everyone together at seven tonight? Erica, you can bring Mike if he'd like to come."

"Yes, and Brian and Leslie will want to be here, too," she reminded them.

"Okay. Alex and I can discuss some of the details now, but we'll make the big announcement tonight."

"Thanks, Dad. Thanks, Alex. I shouldn't be too long." Erica ran for the car.

A few minutes later Becky was sliding into the front seat. "Let's go somewhere we can talk without being seen."

"How about the newspaper office? No one will be there today."

"Good. I hate to sound so mysterious, but I want to help Carolyn without her knowing."

Erica pulled up behind *The Kerusso* building, and the two girls got out. "Let's sit in Dad's office," Erica said as she unlocked the door. "It has the most comfortable chairs."

Once seated, Becky didn't seem to know how to begin.

"Just tell me," coaxed Erica. "Whatever it is, I'll try to help."

Becky drew a deep breath. "The other night I was talking to Carolyn about the Lord. She really wants to accept Him, but it seems like she's afraid to. Anyway, she started to cry and said, 'I can't. God wouldn't have me because I've done something awful.' "

"Did she tell you what it was?" asked Erica.

Becky nodded. "Yes. That's why I'm telling you. You might be able to convince her she can be forgiven."

"Me? I'm just a new Christian myself. And she doesn't like me." When Becky didn't respond, she said, "How can I help?"

"First, I need to know how you feel about her," Becky replied. "I know she was nasty to you at the hayride, and she's been trying to come between you and Mike. Are you interested in helping Carolyn? Not me, but Carolyn?"

Erica hesitated only a moment. "Yes," she said. "Two weeks ago, I may not have been, but . . . well, I'm beginning to care—to feel sorry for Carolyn."

"Why?"

Erica spread her hands. "I realized her home life is probably not as good as mine. Carolyn's mother doesn't seem to care about her and what she does. And so," she added simply, "if I can help her, I'd like to do it."

"Good," said Becky. "You'll need to forgive her and let her know that God is much more willing to forgive."

"Of course," said Erica. "After all, a few angry words and sharing rides with Mike hasn't hurt me that much."

Becky toyed with the lace on her sleeve. "There's more."

"What?"

"It began when a nice-looking man started dating her. She wasn't willing to listen when I tried to tell her he wasn't good for her. She was soaking up all the affection she could get."

Erica sat forward in her chair, waiting for more.

"Somehow, I'm not sure how, he convinced her you were her enemy, that you had done things to hurt her, like stealing a boyfriend."

"I didn't," Erica protested.

"Carolyn thinks you did. A boy she was dating, Arnie Butler, took you out."

"I went out with him once. I didn't even like him."

"Well, Carolyn is convinced that you stole Arnie from her and then stole Mike from me."

"Did I?"

"Of course not. I told you that the night of the hayride. I haven't changed my mind."

"Okay. Go on."

"When this guy had her convinced you were her enemy, he proposed that she harass you with anonymous notes, submissions to the school paper, and snide remarks that others would overhear."

"It *was* Carolyn! I thought so until I met Jerry Palmer. Then I started to change my mind. But why would she do all that just because—?"

"She had more incentive. Every time she left a note or was successful in making you squirm, her boyfriend would buy her a new dress, or coat, or something."

"Oh, poor Carolyn! When did she find out she was being used?"

"That night at the Spaghetti Warehouse. Since you had started being nice to her—not getting angry when she butted in with Mike and things like that—she told the guy she wouldn't do anything more." Becky twisted a ring on her finger. "There was to be at least one more note about the poster evidence being in your trash here at the paper. When she refused, he threatened her."

"With what?"

"Exposure. He said Mr. Tyson would tell your father she was behind it all."

"But he couldn't do that without incriminating himself."

"Carolyn didn't think of that. She had promised to do it, but then she walked out, telling him it was the last thing she'd ever do."

"Good for her. Oh, Becky, I'm glad you told me. Of course I forgive her. I just have to find a way to tell her."

"Thanks, Erica." Becky breathed a big sigh. "I was scared to even ask you this morning until I saw you reach out to her. Then I knew my prayers were answered."

"Carolyn may not be under any more pressure anyway. I was late because Alex thought he'd found proof that Tyson is behind the attack on Senator Palmer and the trouble at the paper."

"I hope he's right. If that's true, perhaps Carolyn will feel able to accept Christ." Impulsively, she jumped up and hugged Erica. "Oh, everything *is* working out well."

Arm in arm, they walked out to the car. After Erica dropped Becky off at her house, she drove home and dashed into the house. "Dad, Alex," she called. "I've got news, too."

"What is it?" asked her father.

"Does it have to do with Tyson and Palmer?" Alex asked.

"Yes."

"Spill it," said Alex.

"I found out this afternoon who left the notes and why."

"I'd like to hear why," said her brother. "I know who. It was Jerry Palmer."

"Wrong. It was Carolyn White. She did it because she was angry with me. Besides, she was paid to do it."

"By whom?" asked Alex, his ever-present notebook and pencil poised.

"By a man she was dating, who—"

"Who is Tyson's henchman," Alex interrupted. "Didn't I tell you?"

"Right. But she didn't know that until the night of Brian's birthday, when she was forced into writing another note. Her boyfriend threatened her that Tyson would tell Dad that she was behind everything."

"That's ridiculous," Mr. Nelson said in disbelief. "She couldn't possibly be the cause of what's happened."

"But it scared her into confessing to Becky."

————

That evening, when everyone had gathered in the rec room, Mr. Nelson stood. "This all began with an editorial meant to inform the people of a bad bill," he said.

"No, Dad," said Alex, taking over the meeting as usual. "It started before that. Remember when Mr. Tyson offered you twice what the paper was worth? You told us about it and wondered why he'd pay so much."

"Yes." Mr. Nelson sat back down.

"I decided to find out. Pete and I began a search to find out who Tyson is and what he would do with the paper if he got it." Alex began to pace as he spoke.

"Next, Mom decided to leave," Alex continued, "and Tyson renewed his offer. You refused, and he threatened you. But, until you wrote that editorial, nothing happened. He didn't carry out his threats."

"That's true," Mr. Nelson agreed.

"The editorial set everything in motion and gave Tyson a chance to act. He got someone, we don't know who, to print the posters, paid Milton to tack them up, then let everyone assume you were responsible for the poster as well as the editorial."

Brian spoke up. "I think he did more than that. He started people thinking that way."

"Right," agreed Alex. "His next step was to threaten various businessmen, warning them what would happen to their businesses if they advertised in *The Kerusso*."

"And I started losing money," interjected Mr. Nelson. "He thought I'd have to sell to him, and for almost nothing. In fact, that was his latest offer—almost nothing."

"But why?" asked Mrs. Palmer. "It seems senseless. Why does he want *The Kerusso*? And why did he want to ruin my husband?"

"I can only guess why he wants *The Kerusso*," explained Alex. "If he controlled the paper, he could hide certain information from the people of this area—information the big papers probably wouldn't carry unless somehow he was exposed."

Senator Palmer shook his head. "What information?" he asked. "I don't understand."

"Information about the land deals he was trying to make. Land deals exactly like the ones that had gotten him into trouble before."

"How does that involve my husband?" asked Mrs. Palmer.

Alex grinned. "Senator Palmer could expose him. The senator knew all about those old land frauds, and he could stop Tyson before he made his money and ran."

Erica looked around the room. Everyone looked as puzzled as she felt. Everyone except Mrs. Palmer. Her face clouded with anger.

"Are you accusing Ralph of complicity?" she snapped.

"No," Alex shook his head. "Just knowledge. Your husband, Ralph Palmer, represented Tyson in similar land deals and got him off," Alex said.

"I never—" protested the senator.

"Yes," Alex insisted. "Remember Mr. Tyler in Bozeman, Montana?"

"Of course, but that's Tyler, not Tyson."

"One and the same." Alex tapped his pencil on his notebook. "I sent for the court records and read through the transcript. If you'll compare the land deal in Bozeman with the prospectus of the Orcas Island deal and the one in Everett, you'll find they are identical."

"Good work, son," said Mr. Nelson. "Is this enough to bring a case against Tyson?" he asked Senator Palmer. "Will it prevent him from going through with the land deal? Keep him from trying it somewhere else?"

"It will," assured Senator Palmer. "You know, a guilty conscience is a funny thing. I would never have tied Tyson to Tyler if he hadn't caused all this furor. I certainly didn't recognize him with that beard. If he'd just gone ahead with his land deal, I'd never have noticed a thing. He could have gotten away with it again."

"He's cost me a lot of money," said Mr. Nelson, "but I guess it's worth it if we can stop him."

―――――――

The next several days passed swiftly. Mr. Tyson was arraigned and let out on bail.

School activities picked up their pace as Erica's class prepared for graduation. Mrs. Nelson promised to be home for the Mothers' Tea.

The Kerusso office hummed. In just a few days all advertisers were back, ordering even bigger ads to make up for lost time. Subscribers flocked back, too, and Erica kept busy processing new or renewal subscriptions.

Thursday night, while Erica was home alone, she pressed the dress she planned to wear to the tea. The phone rang, and she ran to answer.

"Erica?"

"Oh, hi, Mom. Everything all right?"

"I'm afraid not, Erica. The president of the company called a special meeting for tomorrow afternoon. I can't fly home in the morning."

"Oh, Mom . . ." wailed Erica. "The Mothers' Tea!"

"I'm sorry, Erica. There's no way I can miss this meeting."

Erica bit her lip. Tears welled in her eyes. "It's all right, Mom. I understand. And, Mom, remember how I hung up the phone on you a while ago? I'd like to ask your forgiveness."

She heard her mother sigh. "I forgive you, dear. We'll talk more about it this weekend. I'll be home tomorrow night. Tell your father to meet the eight o'clock flight."

"Have a good meeting, Mom . . . and a good flight home."

Erica replaced the receiver and returned to the laundry room. She finished pressing her dress, but without the pleasure with which she'd started.

She shook her head. What was it like for kids whose mothers never got to attend school functions, or those who didn't have mothers? How did they feel? she wondered.

When Mr. Nelson arrived home, Erica hurried upstairs. "Dad, Mom called. She's going to be delayed getting here."

Dad's eyes searched Erica's. "How much?"

"She asked that you meet the eight o'clock plane."

"She'll miss your tea."

"Uh–huh," Erica said slowly. "An important meeting came up, and she couldn't get out of it."

"I'm sorry, Erica. I know you're disappointed."

"Yes. But it isn't the end of the world. In a way, it has its benefits. I started thinking about the kids whose parents can never attend school functions. They must feel . . . oh, I don't know . . . sort of left out."

"How about taking a substitute?"

"You? Much as I love you, Dad, I don't think anyone would believe you're my mother."

"I wasn't thinking of me." He grinned. An impish gleam shone in his blue eyes. "I might be tempted," he said, "but I think you would be less embarrassed if you asked Mrs. Havig. Hasn't she been somewhat of a second mother to you this spring?"

Erica looked up. "Yes. In fact, she's sort of my spiritual mother. She showed me how to become a child of God, and she's teaching me to grow. That's a terrific idea."

Erica gave her father a hug, then dialed the phone. "Ellen? This is Erica."

"Anything I can do?"

"Mom called a while ago and said she couldn't make it home for the Mothers' Tea tomorrow. Would you be free to go in her place?"

"How nice of you to think of me. I'd love to. Are you sure it's all right?"

"Yes. In fact, Dad and I were just discussing how you are my mother, in a way. My spiritual mother."

"Thank you, Erica. I'm honored."

Erica swallowed a lump in her throat. "I'm the one who is honored."

———

Friday evening, Mike and Erica strolled through the park hand in hand.

"Mom enjoyed the tea this afternoon," Mike told Erica. "It was nice of you to ask her."

"I'm glad she went. We had a great time. But best of all, Mike, I think I'm winning a victory with my feelings about my own mother."

"Really?"

"When she called to say she couldn't be here, I didn't get angry. I just felt disappointed. I still can't say I agree with the priorities in her life. They aren't what I'd choose."

"Go on."

"But I know now that Mom is who she is, and I must accept and love her that way—not expect her to be what I want."

"That's my girl."

"Your girl?"

Mike turned and pulled her to him. He held her closely for a long moment, then kissed her. "Yes," he said. "My girl. You will be, won't you?"

Would she? Yes. Her thoughts flashed to Brian. She would continue to pray that his deep feelings for her would change and, most of all, that he—and Leslie—would come to know Jesus.

Teen Series From
Bethany House Publishers

Early Teen Fiction (11–14)

HIGH HURDLES by Lauraine Snelling
Show jumper DJ Randall strives to defy the odds and achieve her dream of winning Olympic Gold.

SUMMERHILL SECRETS by Beverly Lewis
Fun-loving Merry Hanson encounters mystery and excitement in Pennsylvania's Amish country.

THE TIME NAVIGATORS by Gilbert Morris
Travel back in time with Danny and Dixie as they explore unforgettable moments in history.

Young Adult Fiction (12 and up)

CEDAR RIVER DAYDREAMS by Judy Baer
Experience the challenges and excitement of high school life with Lexi Leighton and her friends—over one million books sold!

GOLDEN FILLY SERIES by Lauraine Snelling
Readers are in for an exhilarating ride as Tricia Evanston races to become the first female jockey to win the sought-after Triple Crown.

JENNIE MCGRADY MYSTERIES by Patricia Rushford
A contemporary Nancy Drew, Jennie McGrady's sleuthing talents promise to keep readers on the edge of their seats.

LIVE! FROM BRENTWOOD HIGH by Judy Baer
When eight teenagers invade the newsroom, the result is an action-packed teen-run news show exploring the love, laughter, and tears of high school life.

THE SPECTRUM CHRONICLES by Thomas Locke
Adventure and romance await readers in this fantasy series set in another place and time.

SPRINGSONG BOOKS by various authors
Compelling love stories and contemporary themes promise to capture the hearts of readers.

WHITE DOVE ROMANCES by Yvonne Lehman
Romance, suspense, and fast-paced action for teens committed to finding pure love.

9606